Rocky froge and pointed to the monitor. "Now here's where it gets really interesting," she said. "Watch Cass Lowry carefully as she talks to this guy."

The camera had moved in to a close two-shot of Cass and the silent man. She peered into the hood, trying to meet his eyes. He turned his head, but not before I could see her expression change slightly.

Rocky stopped the tape again. "Right there!" she said. "Did you see her face? I think she ID'd that guy." She ran the tape back and we watched it again. . . .

I sat back in my chair, my shoulder muscles aching with tension. "You're right," I said. "She knew him. I'm sure of it."

The room lights came up. I stood, feeling a bit dizzy. "She lived a little less than six more days," said Rocky, punching the rewind button. "I know the cops don't agree, but I think these clowns killed her. . . ."

MORE MYSTERIES FROM THE
BERKLEY PUBLISHING GROUP...

DEAD AHEAD

BRIDGET McKENNA

BERKLEY PRIME CRIME, NEW YORK

This book is a Berkley Prime Crime original edition, and has never been previously published.

DEAD AHEAD

A Berkley Prime Crime Book / published by arrangement with the author

PRINTING HISTORY
Berkley Prime Crime edition / July 1994

All rights reserved.
Copyright © 1994 by Bridget McKenna.
This book may not be reproduced in whole or in part, by mimeograph or any other means, without permission.
For information address: The Berkley Publishing Group, 200 Madison Avenue, New York, New York 10016.

ISBN: 0-425-14300-7

Berkley Prime Crime Books are published by
The Berkley Publishing Group,
200 Madison Avenue, New York, New York 10016.
The name BERKLEY PRIME CRIME and the BERKLEY PRIME CRIME design are trademarks of Berkley Publishing Corporation.

PRINTED IN THE UNITED STATES OF AMERICA

10 9 8 7 6 5 4 3 2 1

To Doug,
for love and support;

to my children,
for understanding what makes me do it;

and to my family,
for always accepting
the odd one in their midst.

ACKNOWLEDGMENTS

The author would like to acknowledge the assistance of a number of people who helped this book and this writer along the way: Scott Murphy and Shelley Peckinpah Murphy for a blast of inspiration; Jay Sullivan for much expert advice; Don Maass for conviction and confidence; Melinda Metz for aid and comfort; and Marti McKenna for an unending willingness to listen to another writer's problems.

CHAPTER 1

THE SKY WAS SCREAMING BLUE AROUND A BALL OF YELLOW flame, and the air coming through the vents in my car would have been right at home in a convection oven. It was the height of summer in a year without enough rain to stick in your eye, and as I drove through the bone-dry foothills of north-central California, occasionally slowing down for one of those leviathans on wheels they like to call recreational vehicles, I couldn't lose the feeling that if I rolled down my window I would hear the grass crisping.

It wasn't the traditional movie-version weather for a funeral, but that's where I was heading.

The road flattened out enough for me to restart the air conditioning, and I sighed with relief as the first cool air hit my face. A glance in the rearview mirror showed me sweaty red-orange wisps of hair sticking to my face. I brushed them back with one hand, glad for once that my hair looked about the same regardless of what I did or didn't do to it. I may not be glamorous, but at least I'm low-maintenance.

I was a mile from Cedar Ridge when I passed the Forest Service fire station. The sign outside said "Fire Danger: High." Smokey the Bear posed with his hat and shovel, a frown of concern on his friendly, furry face.

Cedar Ridge was a wannabee tourist mecca in the heart of the California Gold Country, where every small town tried

1

to outdo its neighbors in old-timey charm and ready avail-
ability of cheap souvenirs. It was laid out on either side of
Highway 49, a winding two-lane that stretched from Oakhurst
in the south to Grass Valley in the north, with some local
architect's idea of nineteenth-century-style buildings housing
antique malls and gift shops and real estate offices.

Unlike most towns in the gold country, where many original
gold rush–era buildings still stood, the folks in Cedar Ridge
had torn down all their genuine historic landmarks in an effort
to modernize the place back in the '50's. When they caught
on that the tourists were driving through on their way to more
picturesque surroundings, the town cobbled together a face lift
of false fronts and wooden sidewalks and quaint gilded signs
naming everything in sight after some aspect of the California
Gold Rush.

I watched the gilded signs swinging in a hot, dusty breeze
I thankfully couldn't feel. Gold Digger's Pizza went by, followed closely by the Golden Nugget Ice Cream Parlor. The
Fool's Gold Bar & Grill and the Forty-Niner Saloon were
open for business. I yearned for a cold beer, but this wasn't
the time to stop. My faithful Mickey Mouse watch reminded
me I would barely be on time for the burial.

I drove through town at a snail's pace in an endless line of
vehicles. It looked quiet and peaceful in spite of the clots of
sightseers filling up the sidewalks and clogging the intersec-
tions, but I'd just spent a couple of weeks in another charming
little spot downstate, and I knew the kinds of secrets a small
town can hide and still put on a pretty face for outsiders. This
one, it seemed, hid some deadly ones.

Cassandra Lowry, an old school chum of my mother, had
headed north from Los Angeles one day twenty-five years
before with her five-year-old daughter, Nora, in tow and her
life savings in her pocket, and stopped in Cedar Ridge. She'd
bought a piece of land fronting Highway 49 with a little
run-down store on it, in a row of other little stores on little
parcels, and gone into the book business.

My parents and I used to come here to visit every couple
of years while I was growing up. Nora and I were not close
friends, being separated by three years in age and hundreds of

miles in geography, but our interests were similar and we had always enjoyed one another's company.

The Cedar Ridge I remembered from my visits was small and pretty; the air was fresh and the water pure and the people friendly. According to Nora, not that much had changed over the years except for one thing: a few months ago, people started showing up at the main intersection in town wearing white robes and hoods. There were even small children in child-size regalia, passing out hate literature to cars who had to stop at the intersection on their way through town.

Cassandra Lowry had gotten mad. She had spoken out against the politics of hate, and ignored warnings to mind her own business. One night last week Cass had run her car off the road, down into a deep ravine filled with granite boulders. She died on impact. The coroner ruled it accidental death. Nora didn't agree, and called me—Caley Burke, Private Investigator—with exactly one major case under my belt since I had acquired my license only a couple of months before.

Jake Baronian, a shoo-in for sainthood in my book, waved me out the door of Baronian Investigations and said he'd see me soon, though I'd been back at work only about a month following a less-than-peaceful vacation during which I'd had to kill an old friend. "I hope you don't think I'm going to spend all my time chasing auld acquaintance," I told him with an apologetic smile.

"No, I don't. And don't forget to take your gun."

Since the shooting, a hands-down case of self-defense, I had come to look at my familiar Walther PP like I might a kitten that had turned into a venomous snake. Prior to that awful night, I'd never even taken the damned thing out and waved it around, much less pulled the trigger unless I was standing at the pistol range wearing goggles, plugs, and covers. I'd never heard the sound of a gunshot muffled by human flesh, or smelled the scent of blood and gunpowder, a stench I thought I'd never get out of my head even after I could no longer actually smell it.

A week after the shooting, I was back at work up in Cascade, a middle-sized town at the north end of California's Central Valley, where I've worked for Jake Baronian at

Baronian Investigations for a little more than three years. I took to leaving the gun in my desk drawer when I left the office, and Jake took to following me down to my car and bringing it to me.

"It saved your life when you needed it, Burke," he reminded me. "I know how you feel, and I'm not telling you it'll go away, because it won't. But you'll learn how to deal with it. Meantime, take the gun."

So I took it. But I locked it into the glove box of my car where I didn't have to look at it or feel the weight of it against me.

The scattering of buildings along the highway thickened up into a town, and I began looking for the Gold Hill Bookstore, Cass and Nora Lowry's business, where Nora had said she'd be waiting.

I saw the bookstore ahead on my left and looked for an opening in the steady stream of cars and RV's that poured through the town, their occupants gaping out the windows at all the manufactured charm. The interaction of the dozens of small streets and driveways off the main drag, with the distraction of the visitors and the impatience of the locals, made for an interesting traffic situation; sort of a cross between big-city gridlock and rush-hour on the freeway, all in a town without a single traffic light.

I eased my rented Chevrolet between a pickup with a gun rack and a station wagon towing a vacation trailer, and zipped across the oncoming lane into the postage-stamp blacktop that served the store as a parking area. I sighed with relief that I was still alive. Nora was waiting for me at the door.

"I'm so glad you could come," she said, hugging me. Nora was about my size, with short dark hair and dark eyes in a pixie face. She had a husky, almost hoarse quality to her voice that made people turn and look at her the first time they heard her speak, and a direct gaze that belied her many insecurities. I often wished I knew her better, but we lived pretty far apart and had seen one another only once or twice since she came home after college.

"Mom wanted to be here," I told her, "but she's in bed with the flu. She called me right after you did."

Three people came out of the store and stood behind Nora. An older woman in a wheelchair pushed her way to the front of the group and held up her hand. "You must be Caley Burke. I'm Dolores Boyd."

"Dolores was one of Mom's best friends," Nora added. "She owns an antique store here in town. This is Danny Abrahams." She indicated a slender young man with dark, curly hair who stood behind Dolores with one hand resting on her shoulder. We nodded at one another and smiled. "Danny's a writer. He came here from San Francisco a couple of years ago."

Nora had told me that Danny and Dolores had pitched in with her and Peter to cover my fees and expenses while I was here. I had not one but four clients, it seemed.

"And this is Peter McKay."

Peter McKay was a book illustrator who had lived with Cass Lowry for the past four years or so, according to my mother's reports. He was perhaps a few years younger than she had been, with coarse, sandy hair going gray, and intelligent black eyes in a face that would have been right at home on a cowboy. It was a reserved face, weathered and strong. "How do you do, Ms. Burke," he said, clasping my hand firmly, "I'm glad you decided to come down."

Nora's five-year-old twins, Matt and Harry, pushed open the bookstore doors and ran to their mother's side. They looked a lot like her, and a lot more solemn than five-year-olds should ever have to look. One of them took Peter's hand and held it. Peter looked down at the boy and smiled.

We stood around an awkward moment while I wondered whether I should say I was glad to be there, given the circumstances. Nora saved me by closing the door to the bookstore and taking me by the arm. "The cemetery's right across the highway. We're going to walk."

"I'm going to roll," Dolores asserted, and propelled her chair down a ramp and across the parking lot ahead of us. When we reached the highway, she parted cars and trailers like a Red Sea of steel and we followed in her wake. A black hearse waited on the hill, and Peter and Danny joined the men who were pulling a plain black coffin from the back.

"I couldn't see taking a limousine from the funeral home," said Nora beside me. "Mom was never one to stand on ceremony. We used to bring our lunches over here sometimes and eat on the grass. She used to want to be cremated, but she loved this place so much, she changed her mind."

The cemetery was picturesque, with century-old tombstones and fenced plots surrounding a white clapboard chapel. A dozen or so large oaks shaded the patchy grass from the worst of the sun, but the heat was still oppressive.

Back behind the old section was a more modern area with inset markers and plastic flowers, but Cass was being buried between a Bohemian immigrant and his wife who were laid to rest in the early 1900's and two sisters who had died in childbirth the same year, 1881. It gave me a sense of the endless march of life and death, which I didn't really welcome just then.

Others joined us at the graveside, members of the local business community and assorted acquaintances and bookstore customers. Judging by the turnout, Cass Lowry had either been a very popular woman, or else there was nothing else to do around here on a Monday afternoon. A few people wore black in spite of the heat, and there were even a few suits and ties that looked as though they'd been hauled out of storage for the occasion. Sweat stains were much in evidence, and I felt none too fresh myself after the long drive down from Cascade.

There was no priest or minister present, and the burial was performed without undue ceremony. A few people stood up and talked about Cass and her contributions to the community. Dolores and Danny talked about friendship. In the moments of silence in between, I could hear bees going about their relentless business, buzzing something about life going on anyway.

Peter stood quietly, tears sparkling in his dark eyes. No one seemed to expect him or Nora to put their feelings into words. The twins fidgeted, looking up at their mother now and then as if they might find in her face the answer to this sudden change in their lives.

In thirty minutes or so it was over. Nora invited everyone over to the bookstore, where some townspeople had prepared a buffet. I'd been feeling more than a little mortal anyway, since my close scrape on the south coast, and as I walked back across the highway I imagined I could feel some flimsy and insubstantial life substance passing in and out with every breath.

CHAPTER 2

THE BOOKSTORE WAS CROWDED WITH PEOPLE STANDING about in little groups and eating finger foods. Just inside the door a young girl dispensed espresso drinks from the huge copper and brass machine Cass had acquired several years ago when she turned part of the bookstore into a coffeehouse. I accepted an iced latte gratefully and Nora took me around and introduced me to everyone as a childhood friend. I had met a few of them before, but because I'd been too shy as a child and teenager to make much of an impression, they didn't remember and I didn't remind them.

I saw Nora's ex-husband, Eddie Shepard, looking out of his element in a dark suit that fit too tightly on his huge frame. Eddie was a big man, but hadn't gone to fat. He'd always prided himself on being the biggest, strongest, and meanest guy around, and it looked as though he still held the title. I said hello, but like every time we'd met in the past, Eddie and I didn't have much to talk about once the state of the weather had been established. I was grateful when we exhausted that topic and were forced to find other people to talk to.

Most of the people there were strangers to me. I tried to connect the names and faces I was hearing for the first time, knowing I'd be talking to a lot of them again over the next few days, but my mind was back in the cemetery with dead folks, back in a cave on a beach with gunshots ringing in my ears, deep in my own sense of looming mortality, and it was a struggle. I gulped my first latte and sipped my second while watching people offer awkward expressions of sympathy to Nora and Peter. The caffeine kicked in, bringing the usual false uplift and making the circumstances a little closer to bearable.

I looked around at the Gold Hill Bookstore, which Cass had created from next to nothing over the last twenty-five years, and thought that if a person had to die—and let's face it, a person has no choice in the matter—this wasn't a bad thing to leave behind. The summer sun poured through windows and skylights onto wooden shelves and tables of books. Dozens of foliage plants lent a feeling of persistent life.

Matt and Harry played with blocks and toy trucks on a soft rug in the middle of the children's book section, now and again stopping their play to watch the adults transforming the tragedy of their grandmother's death into a quiet social gathering. I could see their confusion, but couldn't offer any help. I didn't pretend to understand the social mechanics of funerals any better than they did.

The coffeehouse portion took up much of the front of the bookstore, with generous square tables of dark wood, each graced with a small vase of fresh flowers, inviting customers to sit and talk awhile. I sat at one of the tables and remembered the bookstore in happier times, with locals and tourists buying books and soaking up the easy atmosphere.

Cedar Ridge was small and insular, despite or maybe because of the constant influx of strangers who stayed an afternoon or a day and left without knowing anything but the surface. The town wasn't known for either refinement or higher education, but many of its citizens were emigrants from more literate climes like San Francisco or L.A., and Gold Hill was a central meeting place for them.

"So you're a friend of Nora's from up north?" A bearded red-haired man was leaning against a nearby shelf of books and grinning down at me with what he probably thought was charm. He held a cappuccino in one hand and a plastic plate of cold food in the other. His face was youthful, but his hair and beard showed more than a few gray hairs.

"I'm Caley Burke," I replied. "I've known Nora since we were kids." I raised an inquisitive eyebrow.

"Mike McCutcheon. I own the big car lot right up the street there." He pointed his drink at the store window, indicating a neatly paved lot in the distance, where red, white, and blue pennants stirred listlessly over a couple of dozen cars. "My real love is restoring classic cars. I've got a collection of American steel you have to see to believe. I'm also the president of the Cedar Ridge Business Association." He balanced the plate on the cup and put out a small hand with a showy class ring on one pinky. "Did you come to town just for the funeral, or will you be staying awhile?"

"A few days," I replied, reaching up and shaking his hand.

"That's great. I'm sure I'll see you around, then." He gave me a wink. "You know, us redheads ought to stick together. I'd really like to show you my car collection sometime. It's all in a great big garage I had custom built next to my house."

"Sounds terrific," I said, picking up my glass. "Well, I'd better go feed the parking meter." I got up and walked away.

"There aren't any parking meters in Cedar Ridge," Mike McCutcheon protested, but I didn't even turn around.

Nora was standing with Peter, Danny, and Dolores among shelves filled with cookbooks on the other side of the room. I headed in that direction.

"I see you've met Mike," a pleasant masculine voice said behind me. "He never wastes much time."

I turned to face a good-looking man of about forty with pale blond hair and extraordinary blue eyes. "He's wasting time coming on to me," I told him, shaking my head. "Definitely not my type."

The man laughed. The blue eyes twinkled. "It wouldn't be the first time he made that mistake, but it never stopped him from trying. I'm Tim Wynand." He held out a hand and I took it. The grip was warm and friendly.

"Caley Burke. I'm a friend of Nora's."

"Will you be staying in Cedar Ridge long, Ms. Burke?"

"I hope not, Mr. Wynand. It seems to be the height of tourist season. And if you're not a tourist, I suspect there isn't much to do around here."

"Well, the main tourist season around here lasts from March till November," he said, "and then we get skiers passing through the rest of the year. To upset a phrase, I wouldn't want to visit here, but it's a great place to live. Real estate is still low, schools are good, and we have an excellent newspaper."

I raised an eyebrow. "Really?"

"Really. The *Foothills Sentinel*. I publish it. I'm also the editor, and I write a lot of the features, and in a pinch I can do most any job on the paper, including advice to the lovelorn." His voice was quiet and Midwestern with a touch of amused self-effacement.

"I'll be sure to pick up a copy while I'm here. Did you know Cass well?"

"She was one of my dearest friends in town. I've only been here about seven years now, and Cass was one of the first people to befriend me." He waved an arm at the cozy surroundings. "We used to sit around this store and talk far into the night about nearly everything. I was in love with her for years. This was all before she and Peter got together, of course."

"Cass was a good friend of my mother's," I told him. "I didn't know her well, but I liked her."

"Everyone did. Even those of us who loved her." He looked at my empty latte glass. "Are you ready for another of those?"

"No thanks. Two's my limit. What are you having?"

He held up a glass of clear liquid adorned with a lime wedge. "Mineral water. Best stuff in the world for you. Unlike alcohol or caffeine, you really *can* quit any time you want."

"Tim! What a surprise!" A tall, dark-haired woman in a hot-pink dress and spike heels crossed the room and joined us.

"I don't know why it should be a surprise. Cass was one of my dearest friends."

"Well, yes, five years ago perhaps, but since she took up with Peter, I thought . . ."

"I doubt it, Maureen," Tim said quietly. His mouth formed into a slight grimace of distaste. She didn't seem to notice.

"I don't think I know your friend," she said, flashing a brief smile in my direction.

"Maureen Adler, Caley Burke. And vice versa." He winked at me conspiratorially. "Maureen is the queen of Cedar Ridge real estate. If there's a real estate big time, she's destined to get there, and soon."

"Oh, Tim, you're such a flatterer." Maureen Adler waved off the perceived compliment with a flick of nylon fingernails and a flutter of synthetic eyelashes. "Pleased to meet you, Ms. Burke. Are you new in town?"

"Just visiting, I'm afraid."

"Oh, don't be afraid—it's a wonderful town! Who knows, maybe you'll like it so much here you'll have to stay." She handed me a glossy pink business card with her name embossed in unreadable fancy script. "And you'll love our prices on homes."

I slipped the card into a pocket. "Thank you."

"Don't mention it. Oh, there's Fletcher Birdsall! I wonder if he's finally ready to sell that old place of his. Ta, Tim. Ms. Burke." She crossed the room and descended on a gray-haired man who looked understandably dismayed to see her.

"Whew!" was all I could manage.

"Maureen has that effect on most people," Tim said. "I don't know how she manages to rack up so many sales."

"Life is full of mysteries," I acknowledged.

"And maybe the greatest mystery of all is how goddamned temporary it is."

The anger in Tim Wynand's voice made me turn and stare. A look of sorrow crossed his boyish features. "It shouldn't have happened to Cass. Not like that." His voice cracked slightly. He let out a deep sigh. "It was good to meet you, Ms. Burke. I hope to see you again while you're in town." He set his glass on an empty table and walked to the door, barely noticing several people who spoke to him on the way out.

I turned around and bumped into a tall woman with long blond hair. Her plate of food spilled on the carpet and I got down to help her pick it up. "I'm so sorry," I said. "I didn't see you standing there."

She smiled. "I was looking for someone," she said. "I didn't see you, either. My name's Judy Roy." She brushed croissant crumbs from her jacket and pants.

"Caley Burke. I'm a friend of Cass and Nora's."

"I'm afraid I didn't know Ms. Lowry well," Judy Roy said, chucking her plastic plate into a nearby wastebasket. "We didn't really have any mutual friends and I don't get into the bookstore all that often. I love to read, but I haven't had much time since I joined the Department." She absorbed my blank look. "I'm a deputy sheriff. I live in Black Mountain, but I work out of the Cedar Ridge substation."

"I guess it must be a pretty quiet beat," I ventured.

"You'd be surprised. Saturday nights can get wild, even in a town this size. Some of these local boys like to get smashed and pick fights in the bars. It can be pretty interesting."

"That's one word for it," I admitted. A thought occurred to me. "Were you by any chance one of the officers on the scene of Cass's accident?"

She shook her head. "I was off duty that night. One of the things I hate about this area is the number of fatal accidents. There are stretches of road around here that are five or six times as deadly as an average piece of California two-lane the same length."

"I had no idea."

"Most people don't. They're too busy looking at the gorgeous scenery to notice, but there are places with rock walls on both sides of the road, long stretches that are too dangerous to pass, nasty drop-offs. . . ." Her voice trailed off. Cass had gone over one of those drop-offs and struck the rocks below. Her car was an almost unrecognizable mass of twisted metal when they brought it up to the highway, and Cass had died on impact.

"I see what you mean. I'll be sure to pay more attention when I'm driving around here."

"I hope you do," she said. "It might save your life."

Nora was motioning to me from across the room, so I excused myself. "If I see you again before I leave town," I told Deputy Roy, "I hope it's unofficially."

"Well, stay out of those saloon brawls," she cautioned me with a smile.

"When the crowd thins out we're going back to the house," Nora said when I joined her. "Peter fixed up a guest room for you upstairs."

"I'd actually planned to get a hotel room. I don't want to be any bother to you."

"You're doing us a favor coming here," said Peter. "We wouldn't have known who else to turn to."

"You're paying me perfectly good money to investigate," I replied. "So it's not all that great a favor."

"It is to us, and we want you to stay at the house if you're okay with the idea. We all have a lot of talking to do about . . . what happened." His eyes pulled away from mine, but not before I saw the fresh tears in them. Danny put a hand on his shoulder and Dolores reached out and took one of his hands.

"So will you stay with us?" Nora asked. "It'll be great to have you at the house again."

"Okay," I said. "I'll be happy to." Dealing with other people's grief isn't the easiest thing I do, and I wasn't sure how sincere I was about the "happy" part, but there was no graceful way to refuse the offer. I managed a smile. Peter smiled back, obviously grateful for my decision.

I'd wanted to distance myself from the personal reality of Cass Lowry's death and stick to the professional details of running an investigation. That would have been the safe way to handle this, and in my present vulnerable state I'd needed to think about my own emotional safety first. Now it was time to take a deep breath and step off that path. Maybe I really was in the wrong line of work, I thought, if I couldn't maintain my balance in the face of a simple little personal mortality crisis.

Okay, Burke, I told myself sternly, you've finally figured out that you're going to die someday. But you're alive right now, and you'd better start acting like it.

CHAPTER 3

"IT WAS THE DAMNDEST THING I EVER SAW," SAID DOLORES. "They were standing out on the corner of Highway 49 and Cedar Avenue, marching around and waving placards and dropping leaflets into car windows. Kay Flanders had called me from the Coffee Pot and said I had to get a look at this, so I went outside and there they were, ugly as the mumps."

"Were they Klan?" I asked her.

"They had A.R.C. embroidered on their robes."

"That's for American Rescue Coalition," Danny volunteered. "Andrew Weiss's organization."

"I'm stumped. I've never heard of Andrew Weiss."

"I wish *we* never had," said Dolores, looking at Peter, who was sitting in a corner of the living room with a drink in his hand. Nora was gone, taking the twins to spend the night with a friend. Dolores had brought her chair close to Danny and me. We were sitting on two long couches that faced one another across a narrow strip of Oriental carpet in front of an enormous stone fireplace. Two gigantic gray-and-white cats napped on the carpet, each occasionally stirring long enough to open one disinterested eye and close it again. These were Grumpy and Dopey, kittens Cass had found wandering in a storm ten or twelve years before. I could never tell which was which and I half suspected no one else could either.

15

There was no fire in the fireplace this time of year, and someone had arranged a clay vase of dried grasses on the hearth. The setting sun came through the high windows and turned the walls to gold. On a side table a book lay open where Cass had left it on Friday. Everyone looked over at it from time to time, but no one wanted to close it.

"So fill me in," I said. "Who's Andrew Weiss?"

"Nobody knows exactly," said Danny. A frown creased his high forehead. "No one's ever seen him. He doesn't do radio or TV or public appearances. His politics are slightly to the right of Ghengis Khan and he writes books about what he thinks is wrong with America and how to fix it."

"I'll bite. What's wrong with America?"

"Too many blacks, Hispanics, Jews, Asians, and uppity women for a start," said Dolores.

"Too many liberals," added Danny. "Too many gays, pro-choice voters, and A.C.L.U. members."

"Too goddamned many people who prefer to think for themselves," said Peter. He got up from his chair and sat down at the end of one of the couches. "Andrew Weiss spews ultraright-wing rhetoric that makes intelligent people sick and plays on the fears of the ignorant. As much of a blow as it is to realize it, lots of people right here in Cedar Ridge are all too eager to believe everything he says."

"He scares the shit out of me sometimes," said Dolores, "but mostly he just makes me mad."

"We thought there might possibly be some A.R.C. activity here in town," said Peter. "We'd seen a few bumper stickers, but no overt activity, so no one knew for sure until they showed up on the corner last April passing out Andrew Weiss hate literature."

"So what happened then?"

"I called Cass and Cass called the Sheriff's Department over at the Cedar Ridge substation," Dolores said. "She asked if they needed some kind of permit to demonstrate, and if they had one. The deputy said they didn't need a permit and that they had deputies on the scene making sure nothing got out of hand."

"Only there wasn't a deputy in sight the whole two hours they were out there," said Danny.

"Or maybe there were, but we couldn't recognize them under the hoods," said Peter.

"Do you really think the Sheriff's Department could be part of something like this?" I asked.

"Not the whole Department, no," said Peter. "I think most of the deputies are ethical, honorable law enforcement officers. But there are some that I suspect would find Andrew Weiss's ideas pretty attractive."

"The fact is," said Danny, "no one saw any sheriff's deputies on the scene. I don't know who Craig thought he was fooling."

"Craig?"

"Craig Bellenger, the deputy she'd talked to," said Danny. "So Cass called back and said where were the deputies keeping order? Some of the people in the cars were throwing the leaflets back out of their windows. Some were even stopping to argue with the A.R.C. guys. It was a Sunday afternoon, all the tourists were trying to get back to the city, and traffic was snarled up at the corner and backing clear down the highway. Still no sheriffs."

"What did he have to say to that?"

"He said he had something important on the other line and hung up," said Peter. He got up and refilled his drink from a bottle on an antique sideboard.

"Cass was mad," said Dolores.

"Actually," said Danny, smiling sadly at the memory, "mad doesn't begin to describe it. She'd lived in this town longer than any of us and never seen anything to make her suspect people around here could actually fall for Weiss's supremacist bullshit. The thought that they had so much support that they could come right out on the street really shook her. She called up a lot of prominent people in town and arranged a meeting. She wanted to do something to fight the A.R.C."

"Cass, Nora, Peter, Danny, and I were kind of the core group," said Dolores. "The gang of five, people called us. And quite a few of the business people joined us, some right away, others when they saw their friends doing it. Danny felt like he oughtn't to be a part of the group at first, and we had to talk him into it."

"Why is that, Danny?"

Danny's green eyes looked evenly into mine. "Well, there's a certain degree of anti-Semitism in an area like this, and homosexuals aren't a real well liked group, either, and that puts gay Jews right down at the bottom of the popularity list. Let's just say I haven't been all that warmly welcomed by the community as a whole, and I thought my presence in the organization might undermine what Cass and the others were trying to do."

So Danny was another target for them. A target—hell, he was practically a one-man minority group. I felt simultaneously relieved to be a part of the faceless northern European white, straight majority and ashamed of that feeling of relief. It had been almost a century since anyone actively excluded or ostracized the Irish, and nobody gave a good goddamn if I moved into their neighborhood.

"Sounds to me like you had a bigger stake in fighting the A.R.C. than anyone," I said.

"Tell that to Gordon Terrell or Billie and Jim Cavanaugh," said Danny. "Gordon's the new veterinarian in town. His kids go to Cedar Ridge High. They've had 'Niggers Get Out' painted on their school lockers, and someone left a fake bomb on Billie and Jim's front porch with a bunch of Weiss pamphlets inside."

"Patty and Martin Chiang have been harassed, too, but not until after they showed support for Cass," said Dolores. "They've lived in town longer than any of us, and thought they were accepted in the community. Now a lot of locals have stopped eating at their restaurant. They can easily stay afloat on tourists nine months of the year, but this winter could be hard on them. And there isn't a goddamned thing any of us can do about all this."

"Cass tried," said Danny. "She loved Cedar Ridge, but she knew that the kind of mindset that's ripe for an Andrew Weiss to come along was always here. She thought it was only a few ignorant people. What really bothered her was the idea that the A.R.C. was so sure of the town's backing that they'd actually come out in broad daylight. After that she devoted every spare minute to gathering support against them."

"Did a lot of the people in town come out for the A.R.C. openly?"

"More than you'd think," said Dolores. "Or at least more than you'd *want* to think. Some even replied to her letters in the paper, defending Andrew Weiss and everyone who follows him. To be fair, a lot of local people were on Cass's side, too."

"It pretty much polarized the town," said Peter. "You could tell a lot of the A.R.C. supporters by who stopped coming into the bookstore. Dolores's business is mostly tourists, and Danny and I are freelancers, but there was a word-of-mouth movement among Weiss sympathizers to boycott the bookstore, and Cass and Nora noticed a difference in the amount of local business they got."

"What all did Cass and the gang do to get on the wrong side of the Weiss crowd?" I asked them.

"Well, there were the letters to the newspapers, and Tim let her do a guest editorial, too," said Dolores. "Tim Wynand owns the *Foothills Sentinel*."

"Yes, I met him this afternoon."

"We also wrote the Cedar Ridge Realty Board and the Sacramento papers," said Danny. "Cass gave a speech in front of the Business Association, pointing out how quite aside from the politics of the thing, an ugly image was bad for business in a town that depended on visitors like this one does. She got in touch with the Klanwatch organization and the Anti-Defamation League, and everyone else she could think of who might be interested."

"She put a petition in the bookstore for people to sign," Dolores added. "And I put one in my store, and some of the other business owners did, too. It was a statement of position against everything the A.R.C. stands for."

"But no direct intervention? No harassment of any kind?"

Dolores shook her head. "At first we were all hot to stop those sons of bitches in their tracks, but Peter educated us a bit on the A.R.C.'s right to demonstrate and what we could and couldn't do to stop them."

I looked at Peter.

"I've had a little experience with political activism," he said.

"Now, Peter, you're being modest," Dolores chided him. "You practically made a career of it when you were younger."

"I knew we couldn't stop them from demonstrating," Peter said. "They had a right to demonstrate peacefully. The Constitution protects everybody—even people we find personally and politically repugnant. I don't think we'd really want it any other way. We couldn't use their tactics against them. We couldn't become the thing we were fighting."

I sighed. "I guess not."

"That was our reaction, too," said Dolores, patting my hand. "We wanted to stomp the A.R.C. and its ideas right into the pavement, but we couldn't infringe on their right to do exactly what they were doing."

"Except when they actually broke the law," said Peter. "By stopping people at the intersection, they were obstructing traffic. If there'd been any sheriffs on hand, they would have had to take some sort of action on that. I told the gang we could be present at the next demonstration—and I was pretty sure there'd be a next one—and watch carefully for any illegal action, no matter how small. If the deputies refused to make an arrest, it would make them look like they were on the A.R.C.'s side."

"And did they come back?" I asked him.

"A couple of months later," he said. "Less than a week before Cass died."

"And did the sheriff's deputies show up this time?"

"They were there," said Danny, "but they didn't do anything, even when the traffic got snarled up there at the intersection. Peter and Cass asked them to take some action on the obstructing traffic thing, but they pretty much told them to mind their own business."

"And there wasn't much else we could do after that," Peter said. "Not without causing more hostility. We'd promised ourselves to avoid direct confrontations with the law. We all had to live here once this was over."

I looked at some notes I had written down in a small spiral notebook. "Nora said that the people who signed Cass's letters to the newspaper all received threats of one kind or another."

"That's right," said Dolores. "There were phone calls and letters in the beginning, but we didn't take them too seriously. We had a head of steam going, and we weren't going to let ourselves be spooked by a bunch of spineless bigots in bedsheets."

"When they saw they weren't scaring anyone off, they escalated the hostilities," said Danny. "Dead animals on the front porch, mutilated baby dolls in the mail. That managed to freak a few people, and they dropped out of the group."

Peter stared at his drink. "Cass said the people making the threats were a bunch of cowards."

"A bunch of *bullshit* cowards," said Nora from the front doorway. She tossed her car keys on the hall table and came over to stand behind Peter. "I believe those were her exact words. She said they'd never have the courage to carry out any of those threats." She shook her head and sighed. "I wish she'd been right."

Peter reached up and squeezed Nora's hand. "No one wishes we could change the past any more than you or I do, Nora, but if we have to face life without Cass, at least I want to know what really happened last Thursday night, and I want to know that whoever's responsible is going to pay." The grief in his eyes was replaced for a moment by a flash of anger.

I cleared my throat. "I might as well get some tough questions out of the way. Why are you so sure Cass's death wasn't an accident?"

"They told her if she didn't back off, she'd be dead," said Danny.

"I know. But a threat might just be a threat. What is it that makes you think they actually did it? Is there any evidence at all for murder?"

Peter hung his head. "Right now it's all suspicions. All feelings."

"But that doesn't mean our suspicions are wrong," said Nora.

"No, it doesn't," I agreed. "We might be able to uncover something as we go along. It's hard enough for one person to get away with murder—if a whole group is involved, sooner or later someone's going to crack. Was there any sort of police investigation?"

"After Cass's death was declared accidental, the Sheriff's Department told us there was no reason to investigate," said Peter. "We asked for the investigation to be continued, but they said there was no evidence. Or rather that all the evidence there was pointed to accidental causes." He sighed. "I'm just not buying it."

"None of us are," said Danny.

I looked at all their faces and met looks of stubborn determination that seemed to dare me not to believe. I wouldn't know what to believe until I'd uncovered some facts.

I turned my notebook to a blank page and picked up a pencil. "If Cass was deliberately run off the road, there's some evidence somewhere," I told them. "We just have to find it."

It was nearly midnight when we finished talking, with quite a few leads for me to follow and quite a few blanks still to be filled. Danny and Dolores left in Danny's car. Nora and I watched the taillights disappear down the long driveway and turn onto the dirt road, then climbed the stairs to the guest room, leaving Peter pouring himself another drink in the darkened living room.

CHAPTER 4

· · · · · · · · · · · · · · · · · ·

THE GUEST ROOM WAS LOVELY AND WELCOMING, WITH DARK green and rose colors against a background of pale cream, totally unlike the hunting lodge atmosphere of the big room downstairs. There was a raised bed platform and a sitting area with an overstuffed chair and a floor lamp next to a tall shelf of books. I thought about my sparsely furnished and largely undecorated studio apartment up north, and I wanted to move in here and stay.

Peter had carried my luggage up earlier and it waited for me at the foot of the bed. I opened the suitcase and took out some clothes and hung them in a closet that smelled of cedar. It was all so damned homey, a feeling I always seemed to have in other people's houses and never in my own, possibly because I grew up being dropped into a place and then pulled out again before I could feel like I belonged there. My parents had a restless wanderlust I never shared. Now I'd lived in the same middle-sized town for almost fourteen years and still hadn't made it my home. Maybe I didn't know how.

There was a light knock at the door and Nora stepped in wearing a long green bathrobe and carrying fluffy cream-colored towels and a bar of tissue-wrapped soap. "The bathroom's through this door," she said. "And I see you've found the closet. If there's anything you need, just ask for it."

"I can't imagine needing anything. This is perfect." Dopey, or maybe Grumpy, had followed me up the stairs and was now curled up at the foot of the bed, awaiting attention. I sat down and scratched his head and he rewarded me with a contented grunt.

"We'll probably go out for breakfast whenever we all get up and moving," said Nora. "Peter usually cooks, but I don't want him to do anything but heal for a while."

"He seems lost, doesn't he?"

Nora nodded. "More than any of us." She sat down on the other side of the bed, still holding the towels. "I think you always know you'll lose your parents someday. It's something you expect somehow, though God knows I never expected it so soon." Her voice grew even huskier. "For Peter, though, I think it's even more of a shock. He expected to be with her the rest of his life."

My parents are still relatively young and healthy. We seldom agree on matters of any importance, particularly politics, and don't see one another often. I silently wished them long and peaceful lives. "Will Danny and Dolores be coming along?" I asked, partly to change the subject.

Nora set the towels down on the bedside table. "Probably not Dolores. She has her antiques store to open, and her clerk doesn't come in until noon. Danny's schedule is a little more flexible. I'll call both of them first thing in the morning and see what we can arrange."

She looked into my open suitcase at the picture that was lying on top of my clothes. "Friend of yours?" she said, holding the picture up to the lamplight.

I nodded. "Good friend. His name's David Hayden. He's a painter, and he lives on the south coast, in Morado Beach."

Nora shook her head, smiling. "And you're still way up in Cascade?"

"David means a lot to me," I said, looking at the photo, which I'd taken the day I left Morado Beach a little more than four weeks ago. David stood on the beach, his hands in the pockets of his jeans, white shirt open at the neck. The blue surf was behind him, the sun bringing out golden highlights in his dark hair. "The feeling's mutual. But he's got obligations down there, and I've got my job up north. . . ."

Nora put the picture frame on the night stand. "I guess it's hard for me to understand how you could pass up the chance for a relationship."

"Well, we have a relationship, sort of," I protested.

"With him down there and you up in Cascade? How do you plan to make that work?"

It was a tough question, and I realized I'd been avoiding asking it of either David or myself. We hadn't seen one another for fifteen years when I went back to Morado Beach this past spring. We'd gotten reacquainted while I worked on a case for his family, then spent an extraordinary week together after the case was concluded.

After that, David went back to his studio and his grand-father, whom he lived with and cared for, and I went back to my job. We wrote and talked on the phone and planned to visit one another, but never spoke of permanence, though we talked circles all around it. Was permanence really what I wanted? I hadn't let myself stop and give it too much thought.

"We've worked out an arrangement that suits us for now," I said, and hoped I believed it.

Nora placed the picture on top of the stack of towels. "That's good," she said. "I hope it works out for you. My experience with romance of any kind is pretty limited. You probably remember I left here after high school and went to college in Sacramento. I never thought I'd be back, but after I graduated, I couldn't make up my mind what to do next. So I stayed here and married Eddie Shepard. I think you know what a mistake that turned out to be."

Eddie was a macho charmer with lots of animal sex appeal and not much else going for him. Stories I'd heard from Nora suggested a violent temper that seemed to rule his life. To his credit, he never took it out on Nora or the boys, preferring to get drunk and fight in bars.

Eddie'd had every bone in his face broken at one time or another, and all the knuckles on his right hand, and although he spent a few nights in jail and a few more in the emergency room, he seldom looked as bad as the guy who had pissed him off. I always thought Nora deserved something better. Eventually, she figured that out.

Nora hugged a throw pillow and gazed past the walls of the bedroom. "I guess there's still a part of me that thinks I'd drop it all for the right man. I don't know who the right man is, but I'm pretty sure he's not in Cedar Ridge."

"So why haven't you left?"

"I think I'm scared to set out on my own. There are hard decisions involved, and I've always shied away from hard decisions." She shook her head, seemingly annoyed at her own uncertainties. "It was easy to move back in here and go to work at the bookstore. No difficult choices involved at all. I always loved the store—I guess it's mine, now." She sighed heavily. "I'm not sure how I feel about that, either. I like to daydream about a stranger coming through town and falling instantly in love with me and saving me from having to make my own choices." She turned to me with a wry smile. "It's not easy being a grown-up."

Nora stood up and took a battered paperback book from the pocket of her robe. "I think you probably ought to read this," she said, handing it over with a frown.

I took the book. The cover featured an American flag and bold black lettering. *Let's Bring Back America*, by Andrew Weiss. I looked up at her.

"This is the book that started all the fuss," she said. "I estimate at least half the people in town have read it, and I'm afraid to guess how many believe what's inside."

"What *is* inside?"

"Andrew Weiss's prescription for a better country," Nora said. "Scary stuff. Oh, it's all very calmly presented and rational-sounding advice on the ills of society, but his cure is worse than the disease. I think what makes him so attractive to so many people is how intelligent he seems underneath it all. He's not ranting and raving, he's just methodically presenting a philosophy of hate and exclusion." She shuddered visibly. "He's a competent writer, but so was Hitler."

I set the book down. "I probably will have to read it," I admitted, "but not tonight, I think."

After Nora left I walked around the room for a few minutes picking up books and examining the pictures and accessories. I was physically exhausted but mentally far too alert to fall asleep. I pulled out my notes and looked them over.

Cass Lowry had managed to get more than a dozen influential business people on her side to speak out against the American Rescue Coalition, and more than two hundred townspeople had signed the statements displayed in Cedar Ridge business establishments that came out against the politics of Andrew Weiss and his followers.

Nora said she thought more people would have backed them but for fear. In a town this small, a lot of the locals were bound to know people who were associated with the A.R.C., and nearly as likely to be related to them. Not a few people had expressed sympathy for what they were doing, but refused to put their names on a piece of paper that might be used against them somehow.

Even before Andrew Weiss came along, and that had been only a few years ago, there had always been some people who had belonged to or supported other organizations similar to his. The difference was that in those days there were no demonstrations and no campaigns for public support. Many locals and a lot more immigrants from the big cities to the South and West had lived here for years without dreaming this scenario in their worst nightmares. When the nightmare came, Cass Lowry had decided to stand her ground.

Cass had always been long on determination, I remembered; it was what got her out of a bad marriage in Los Angeles, took her hundreds of miles from anything she knew, and got her a business that would grow and support her and her daughter. Now her determination not to let hate and ignorance rule her adopted community had possibly gotten her killed.

I sighed and closed the notebook. Tomorrow I'd take a look at the police reports. I didn't expect to run up against any official barriers, since the case was officially closed, but I also didn't expect to learn much of use. There wouldn't be any conspicuous evidence of wrongful death in the reports; if there were, it wouldn't have been ruled accidental. If a break was coming my way, it would probably depend on unofficial information, stories, rumors, little lies and inconsistencies that surface when you've asked the right questions over and over.

That's what my job was all about—going over the same ground ad nauseam and hoping for a little flash of insight. Right then I'd have traded it all to be able to fall asleep. I tossed the notebook onto the night stand, changed for bed, and put the rest of my things into drawers. I scanned the shelves and chose a book calculated to bore me into unconsciousness, but eventually I had no choice but to turn out the light and think about death.

CHAPTER 5

THE COFFEE POT WAS A POPULAR BREAKFAST HANGOUT IN Cedar Ridge. It was decorated like an old-fashioned kitchen, with lots of blue and white tile and antique woodstoves and copper pots hanging everywhere. The smoking section, a sunny dining room facing the highway, was mostly crowded with locals and European tourists, creating vast clouds of smoke that billowed up to the ceiling. Nonsmokers were exiled to a smaller and darker back room. I've noticed it's easy to tell whether or not the owner of a restaurant smokes by which group gets shoved into the corner.

Danny and Nora and Peter and I sat around an oak dining table in the Coffee Pot's back room, talking and waiting for a server. Dolores hadn't been able to find anyone to come in this morning to relieve her at the antiques store, but she promised to join us tomorrow. I'd never had quite such a crowd of people to report to before, but they seemed to get along wonderfully, and I liked them all a lot.

A slender middle-aged man in a plaid cowboy shirt, blue jeans, and a white apron came over to the table. "You folks mind if I sit with you a while?" Without waiting for a reply, he pulled up an empty chair between Nora and Peter, turned it around and straddled it, leaning his arms against the chair back.

"Of course not, Tom," Nora told him. "Caley, this is Tom Flanders, the owner of the Coffee Pot."

"Owner, manager, chief cook and bottle washer, that's me," said Tom, holding out a bony hand for me to shake. "Welcome to the best restaurant in Cedar Ridge." He smiled at me with yellowed teeth.

I remembered Tom from the funeral, where he had given a little speech about Cass. He'd been one of the business people who'd joined up with Cass in the fight against the A.R.C., and put one of the gang's petitions on the counter of his restaurant. "I'm very pleased to meet you," I said.

"Caley's going to stay in town a few days and talk to anyone who might be able to help us determine what really happened to Mom," Nora told Tom. "She's a private investigator."

"Is that so?" Tom's eyes widened. "I don't think I've ever met a private eye before." He looked me over for a moment, then turned back to Peter. "I thought we knew what happened to Cass, Peter. She lost control of her car and went off the road. Are you trying to say it was something else?"

"Everyone knows how she died, Tom," said Peter. "The question is, what happened just before she went through that guardrail? Was she the only car on the road?"

"Well, don't you think if there'd been a witness, they'd have reported the accident and tried to help?" Tom looked puzzled.

"Not if they caused the accident in the first place."

Tom leaned back on the chair and appeared to take all this in slowly. Finally, he spoke. "So you really think someone deliberately ran Cass off the road."

"Yes, we do," Peter answered. "Cass had those A.R.C. creeps worried. They threatened her life more than once if she didn't back off, and being Cass, she didn't. What does it look like to you?"

"Well, I guess I have to agree with you, Peter," said Tom, running his fingers through his graying hair, "but it scares the shit out of me, if you want the truth. I mean those guys threatened *me* a time or two, you know."

Nora put a hand on Tom's shoulder. "Yes, they did. And

you didn't back down like a lot of other people. You were behind Mom all the way."

"Yeah," he said distractedly. "I was right behind her." He snapped to attention, focused on Peter. "Do you have any proof of all this?" he asked. "What I mean is, how scared should I be? Are they going to be going around killing people who were against them?"

"No, we don't have any proof. Yet. That's what Caley is here to find. As for the other, I honestly don't know, Tom. It's been four days now, and there hasn't been any more trouble, but I'd advise being careful for a while."

Tom gulped and nodded. "You can bet I will be, Peter. I'll be extra careful." He stood up. "Now let's see about getting you folks some breakfast."

A pale blond woman in an apron came up to the table. "Tom, did you want me to take this order?"

"Why don't you just give me that order pad, and I'll take care of it myself."

The woman looked uncertain. She held the pad and a ball-point pen and made a helpless gesture as though unsure of what to do.

"You can go on back," Tom said, taking the pad and pen from her grasp. "It won't hurt me to play waitress this once. It's not like I didn't used to do everything around here when this was just a little hole in the wall twenty years ago."

The woman smiled timidly at us as she backed out of the room. "Okay, Tom," she said. She watched us from the open kitchen door for several seconds, then walked into the kitchen, letting the door swing shut.

"Well, what will you have this morning?" Tom inquired, order pad open and pen poised. "Everything's good all the time, of course, but I think the ham and cheese omelette is especially fine this morning—I had one myself. And the home fries are the best in the state."

Armed with these recommendations, we placed an order, and Tom ran it into the kitchen. He was back in seconds flat. This time he moved his chair around to sit beside me. "You know, I was the first one to see those American Rescue guys standing out there on the corner," he said. "I told

Kay something had to be done about it—yes, sir. Kay called Dolores Boyd over at the Antique Barn and Dolores called Cass.

"There was this big meeting the next night, and most all the business people came. Cass wanted to fight them, but some of the store owners just up and left when it came time to sign up."

"Such as who?"

"Oh, I don't know—it probably doesn't mean anything. It's just that a few people left early."

"Try to remember who left early. It could be important."

Tom looked uncomfortable. He stared at the table, then at his hands, then at me. I waited.

"I just don't know how smart it'd be to start naming names," he said finally. "It's not like I don't want to help."

"I know you want to help, Tom," I told him, putting a reassuring hand on his arm. "The people who left may not have been associated with the American Rescue Coalition at all. They may just have been afraid to get involved. You know how that is sometimes."

"Well I wasn't afraid to get involved," Tom said, drawing himself up. "I was one of the first to sign up for the fight—Nora can tell you. Me and Dolores and Molly Sherer were the first three to sign that letter to the *Sentinel*." He stood up. "I've got to get back to the kitchen and keep an eye on things," he said. "I hope I see you again while you're in town, miss." He didn't walk away, but hovered nervously just behind me.

"I'm sure you will, Tom," I told him over my shoulder. It was obvious I wasn't going to get any more out of Tom Flanders on the subject of who had refused to protest the activities of the A.R.C. He was running scared now that the possibility of murder had been raised, and I wasn't sure I blamed him. He had mentioned someone named Molly Sherer, a name I didn't have yet. I took out my notebook and wrote it down. "Who's Molly Sherer?"

"Molly owns a bed and breakfast about a mile up the highway from here," Nora told me. "She had to pull out of the group when her children were threatened."

"You were right in the thick of the gang all along," I said. "Did anyone threaten *your* kids?"

"No. I don't know how I'd have handled it if they had."

"Property damage was another popular motif," said Danny. "Especially if there weren't any children to threaten. When the spooky phone calls and dead kittens didn't scare everyone off, there was a lot of middle-of-the-night spray-painting and window-breaking."

"Somebody threw a rock the size of your head through my front door window," said Tom, pointing through the doorway at the spot. "They did it before the place opened, and I came in and there was all this glass everywhere. I guess I'm lucky they didn't pick the dinner rush."

"A lot of the original group faded when they had to replace a few windows," said Danny, "or listen to phone callers who knew their children's names. I don't guess I can blame them much. Tom hung in, though."

"Did they threaten you?" I asked Danny.

"They did more than threaten," said Nora. "Danny was attacked by a bunch of guys wearing hoods, when he was coming back from a meeting at our house."

"No shit?" I exclaimed. Cass's murder might be speculation, but a genuine assault and battery took the Andrew Weiss crowd out of the peaceful political demonstration arena and put them smack into the criminal belt.

Danny shrugged. "They called me the usual names and tried to hurt me," he said.

"Tried?"

"Self-defense is a sort of hobby of mine, for obvious reasons. Gay-bashing isn't limited to small towns, or to anywhere, for that matter—I've had to defend myself before. These guys couldn't have been too serious or I wouldn't have been able to scare them off by bruising them up a little."

I turned a page and scribbled another note. "Has anyone else been physically attacked?"

"Gordon Terrell," said Peter. "He's a veterinarian who moved to town last year with his two teenage children. Some guys jumped him in the parking lot of the vet hospital late one night. He pulled a gun on them, and they scattered."

"And no one ever got a look at their faces?"

"I wanted to get the hood off one," said Danny, "but I was too busy. There were five of them and one of me. I don't think Gordon saw anything he could identify, either."

"That's the awful part," said Nora. "We don't know who they are. I can't look at people I've known all my life now without wondering if they're a part of it. The people who killed my mother could be having breakfast at the next table and I wouldn't know it."

We all turned involuntarily to look at the next table, where a man and woman sat with their three children. There had even been children, Nora had told me, wearing robes and hoods and handing leaflets full of bigotry and hate to passers-by. I began to get an idea of the kind of justified paranoia she and Peter and the rest had been living with for months. My breakfast arrived, but I didn't have much appetite.

It was only 10 A.M., and the temperature was already racing for ninety. Tourists flooded through town on their way to cooler towns higher up, pausing here and there to gawk and spend money. As I drove through Cedar Ridge I saw block after block of clothing stores, cafes, and gift shops selling phony Western charm along with their other wares. Genuinely old houses had been transformed into quaint bed and breakfast inns, and even the professional buildings were built or refitted to look like refugees from the preceding century.

I passed the Forest Service station again. The sign now read: "Fire Danger: Very High." I didn't envy Smokey his job.

CHAPTER 6

THE CEDAR RIDGE SHERIFF'S SUBSTATION WAS ANOTHER false-fronted Western fantasy that fit right in with everything around it. Most of the official cars in the lot were husky four-wheel-drive vehicles with crash cages and muscular tires perfect for boony-crashing in the mountains. I had called ahead and talked to someone about getting a look at the accident report; now I walked inside and faced a long counter behind which a young deputy in khaki tan shuffled papers into stacks with a distracted air.

"Are you Deputy Hughson?"

The deputy looked up at me and nodded. He was a big boy, a bit beefy—a high-school football star after a few years of home cooking. The buttonholes on his uniform shirt strained a bit against the pull of his belly. "I am, or I stole this name tag," he said, smiling at his joke.

"My name's Caley Burke. I called earlier about the accident report."

Hughson frowned. "Oh, yes, ma'am," he drawled. He searched through the piles on his desk. "It should be in here somewhere." He looked up again. "Did you say you were a private investigator?"

"That's right."

"May I see your license?"

"Certainly." I knew it made absolutely no difference, but I wasn't here to pick a fight with the local law enforcement agencies. I dug for my wallet and pulled out the little rectangle of pasteboard that allows me to practice my profession in the State of California. "Here it is."

Deputy Hughson looked at the license. He read all the writing and turned it over and examined the reverse. "I've never seen one of these before," he said. "So I wouldn't know the real thing from a phony."

"Well, this one's the real thing," I assured him. "I'm working for Nora Lowry."

"Okay." He flipped the license onto the counter. "Why don't you have a seat over there in the waiting area and I'll bring the file over as soon as I find it."

I sat down on a wooden chair opposite the counter and Hughson reached for the phone and turned his back to me while he talked with someone in low, hurried tones. "Okay, okay!" he said finally, his voice rising with excitement so that I could make out the words. "I'll give it to her! You just remember what I told you!" He hung up the phone and picked up a file folder off the top of a stack. He walked it to the counter and slapped it down.

"Thanks, Deputy Hughson," I said, getting up and taking the file. "You've been very helpful."

"Don't take it out of the room," he said, a scowl creasing his big baby-face.

"I wouldn't dream of it." I crossed my heart solemnly with a forefinger, which wasn't the finger I had in mind for Deputy Hughson at all. Taking a seat at a beat-up wooden table near a window that looked out onto a landscape of pines and firs and dry summer grasses, I spread out the contents of the file.

The official Sheriff's Department report on Cass Lowry's fatal accident was pretty cut and dried, as such things tend to be. Official reports don't give a good goddamn that a person was once alive, once loved, once needed by others. Once you're down there on paper as "the deceased," it's all facts and figures.

Cassandra Louisa Lowry, age 51; hair: brown/gray; eyes: blue. Official time of death: 11:53 P.M., June 27th, as called by a paramedic at the scene. Died on impact when her automobile left the road on a particular curve near a particular mile marker and came to rest in a tangle of broken brush and pitiless granite. I wrote down times and places and names.

There was a Medical Examiner's report attached, and I took a deep breath and dove in. It told me nothing I needed to know, and a great deal I didn't want to. Death was instantaneous, caused by impact with a granite boulder which had come through the windshield. Ruling: Accidental Death.

When I was through looking and taking notes, I replaced everything in the folder and dropped it onto the counter on my way out. Deputy Hughson never even looked my way.

As I made the turn onto the highway, I glanced into my rearview mirror. A sheriff's car was pulling out behind me. No reason it shouldn't, but I thought I'd see how long it stayed there. I tried to get a good look at the face under the uniform cap, but the face was in shadow and remained anonymous.

Armed with a Chamber of Commerce tourist map, I took a roundabout route to my next stop, the Big Grizzly Towing Company. The first person on the scene had been a tow-truck driver, who had called the ambulance. I could get to his place by the most obvious route, but that wouldn't tell me if I was being followed, and it didn't seem unlikely, given what had transpired at the Sheriff's Department—Deputy Hughson's behavior on the phone seemed a bit extreme on the subject of me and a few files on an accidental death.

The car stayed behind me until I turned into the dirt and gravel driveway of the towing yard. As it continued down the road, I turned to get a better look at the driver. The profile seemed feminine, the curve of jaw line and neck too gentle for a man's physiognomy. There was no long blond hair in evidence and I couldn't be sure, but it looked like Deputy Judy Roy.

"Can I help you, ma'am?" An enormous copper-skinned man in coveralls wiped his hands on a faded shop rag as he walked out of the darkness of the garage into the sunshine. He was a whole lot more than six feet tall, and his impressive mass looked to be more muscle than fat. It was easy to see why he'd choose a grizzly bear to represent him.

"Are you Kingdom Neary?"

"That's my mama's fault, but yes, I am." His black eyes sparkled with gentle humor.

"Mr. Neary, my name is Caley Burke." I handed him one of my cards from Baronian Investigations. He regarded it with interest, looking from the words to the person in front of him and nodding a sort of approval. It occurred to me that I might very well be the only private investigator most people in Cedar Ridge had ever seen. "I understand you were the first person on the scene of Cassandra Lowry's accident last Thursday night."

"Why don't we go into my office," Kingdom Neary said, pocketing the card and wiping sweat from his wide forehead with a red bandanna. "It's hotter than shit out here."

"You've got that right," I told him.

He turned and walked toward the building. A thick black braid hung halfway down his back, tied with a strip of bright red leather. He had an easy, rolling walk that said he was at ease with himself and his surroundings.

It's interesting to note the differences in the way people occupy space. Some tall people seem almost apologetic about the amount of vertical space they're taking up, almost as though some better use might be made of it. This was not the case with Kingdom Neary. He inhabited his oversized chunk of the universe as though it were barely large enough to contain him.

He led the way into a small cluttered room off the garage where a rotating fan pushed some hot air around, and sat down in a cracked and dirty fiberglass chair behind a desk, gesturing me to a nearly identical chair on the other side. He had saved the best seat for guests, I noted. This one was very nearly clean, and only slightly cracked.

"Would you like something to drink?" he asked. He reached out and pounded the side of a battered soda machine next to the desk. A frosty can fell into the chute and he offered it to me. I accepted gladly. It was cold and sweet and delicious.

He procured a can for himself by the same method, opened it, and took a long drink. "I was coming down that stretch of Forty-nine between Cedar Ridge and Black Mountain," he said without preamble. "I'd been on a Triple A call to get some idiot's keys out of his car up on the Black Mountain Road and I saw in my headlights where somebody'd gone through a guardrail. I stopped the truck and went down and took a look. There was this little white car down there, all smashed to shit."

"Cass Lowry's car."

"Yeah, only I didn't recognize it right away on account of it was demolished."

"So you went down to check it out?"

"First I called an ambulance from my truck, 'cause whoever was in there was either dead or needed a doctor—I could tell that much from the side of the road. Then I went down. They must've been waiting with their foot on the gas down at the Emergency Center, 'cause that ambulance was there in about two minutes flat, and the sheriffs arrived before that. It was already too late, though."

"Was Ms. Lowry dead when you got there?"

"Oh, yes, ma'am, she died on impact, that's for sure."

I had seen the photos and knew he was right. No one could have survived even a few minutes with injuries that massive. Until then I had clung to a shred of hope that she had hung on long enough to say something to someone—a few words that would give me something to go on.

The radio squawked. Kingdom Neary listened to the unintelligible static crackle for a moment, then rose to his feet. "Got a call," he said, offering me a meaty hand to shake. "Sorry I couldn't be more help."

CHAPTER 7

. . . .

I DROVE BACK TO THE GOLD HILL BOOKSTORE AND PARKED
the Chevy in one of the spaces in front. A dark blue sedan
pulled in next to me, and a slender dark-haired man with
pale gray eyes and a face like a hatchet looked over at me
and nodded. I got out of the car and went inside, uncertain
whether mountain etiquette required me to nod back.

Nora was helping a clerk check in a shipment of books. She
waved at me from a waist-high stack of boxes. "I'll be with
you in a minute," she promised. I walked up the steps to the
coffee bar.

Peter sat at a table in the far corner, drinking an iced tea.
I ordered an Italian soda and sat down across the table from
him. He looked at me expectantly.

"We're just getting started," I told him. "We can't hope to
find out everything the first morning. I'll be talking to a lot
of people around town."

"I think some of them will be lying to you," he said.

"Don't think that's going to surprise me," I assured him.
"But the more questions I ask, the more I expect to find out,
even if some people are trying to hide something. Lies have to
be kept consistent, and that's not as easy as it sounds." I sat
back in my chair. It was pleasant to relax for a few minutes
in the coolness of the store, but Peter's presence made me

vaguely guilty about not being back out there uncovering a murder plot.

"Do you enjoy doing this?" he asked.

I cocked my head, uncertain what he meant. I certainly enjoyed sitting around air-conditioned coffeehouses, but was less certain how much pleasure there was to be had creeping along California Highway 49 stuck between hundreds of cars going too slow and stopping too often while the outside temperature tried to make it to three digits.

"The detective business. Do you like it?"

"Some of the time. When it's going right, it's a kind of rush—like the sensation of finding all the right pieces to finish a jigsaw puzzle. Most of the time the metaphor is closer to beating your head against a concrete wall."

The coffee bar attendant brought my soda. Peter waved my money off and paid for it. "So why do you do this for a living instead of, say, being an artist?" he asked me.

Nora had evidently told Peter about my artistic leanings. So far, I'd declined to make a career of it, but I still sketched a lot in my spare time, and was taking classes from an art teacher up in Cascade. "Not good enough yet," I replied. "It's possible I never will be, but I try. I even improve, gradually."

"Did you bring a sketchbook?" he asked.

"I'm never without it anymore," I told him. "Self-expression has always been a problem for me. Drawing's one way of getting around that. If I didn't draw, I might have to consider finding a psychiatrist."

Peter nodded. "I have that feeling sometimes. Danny says the same thing about writing. He says maybe truly sane people steer clear of creativity because it frightens them. I think they avoid it because they *can*. Anyway, I'd like to see your sketches sometime."

Nora came and sat down with an iced latte. I filled her and Peter in on what I'd found out so far, leaving out the gruesome details of the official reports. "I'll be a couple more days just talking to people around town," I told them. "So far, I've encountered one helpful individual and one asshole."

"Anyone we know?" Nora asked.

"Kingdom Neary at the Big Grizzly Towing Company was very helpful. He was the first person at the scene."

"Yes, I know," said Nora. "And the asshole?"

"A sheriff's deputy named Hughson."

"Johnny Hughson. God, what a jerk," said Nora, nodding. "Friend of Eddie's, if that tells you anything."

"Well, most small towns aren't crazy about strangers poking into their business, so I guess I ought to expect a little opposition."

"I wish I could help you friendly up to the locals a bit," said Nora, "but ever since the A.R.C. appeared, I can't look at any of them without wondering if they were one of the people under the hoods. When a customer comes in, unless it's one of the gang or one of our supporters or a tourist, I go into the office and let the clerks handle them."

"It must be awful for you," I said. "This is practically your hometown."

"For all practical purposes, it *is* my hometown. I can barely remember life in Los Angeles. In my mind it's all mixed up with the Emerald City of Oz. I've been in this town and around these people as long as I can remember, and suddenly they're all strangers to me. It's got me a little crazy."

"Maybe you should take a few more days off and stay home," Peter suggested. "You have enough help to cover all the hours the store's open. You don't owe your life to this place, and Cass wouldn't want you to make yourself sick."

"Thanks, Peter, but when I'm not here my mind is racing all over the place. What happened to Mom? Who did it? Is it someone I've known all my life? Someone I liked and respected without knowing what they really were?" Her voice gave out and she sat there with her hands around her glass, gathering herself back up again.

"I know," Peter said. "I know what it's like."

"Of course you do," Nora got up and kissed Peter on the cheek. "Don't worry. I'll deal with it. When we find out who's responsible I'll feel a lot better." She stepped down into the bookstore and walked back to the office.

"It won't always be this awful," I said to Peter, watching Nora's back retreating across the store, "but I guess it's useless to say that now."

"I know it takes time to get distance on something like this," Peter said, staring into his glass. "I've had some practice. I lost a son six years ago. He was fourteen. I still miss him every day, but I don't feel like tearing the whole world to pieces because it was my boy who had cancer."

He looked up at me. "That's exactly how I felt for a long time. My marriage ended right after that. Maybe my anger was to blame, or maybe hers, or maybe we were through before Joe got sick, I don't know. I drank a lot and tried to stay unconscious the first year, and when I woke up I closed up the house in San Francisco and came here."

"What was here?"

He shook his head. "It wasn't *there*. I wasn't drinking anymore, but I was still running. Danny and Elias were my next-door neighbors, and their friendship kept me sane, more or less. They thought I might be better off in a different environment. They were right. Eventually, Danny moved here, too."

"What happened to Elias?"

"He's dead."

More dead people. The room felt crowded with them, invisible and uninvited; the dead of my life and Peter's and Danny's. The dead outnumber the living, someone once said, and their numbers are increasing daily. I took a deep breath and tried to bring myself back to the here and now.

"I get the feeling your work has been tough on you," Peter said. He pointed to my face. "Are those scars job-related?"

I reached a finger up to feel my right cheekbone which until a couple of weeks ago had sported a butterfly bandage. The small straight scar was still red and still surprised me when I looked in a mirror. "This came from being backhanded by a gun butt. There was this guy who was determined to kill me. Someone killed him first." My insides twisted at the recent memory of that encounter.

"This one," I said, fingering a long, thin scar just above my left eyebrow, "came from being thrown against a pier railing in an explosion. No one was trying to kill me that time—I just happened to be in the neighborhood when they were trying to kill someone else." That wound had been a bit messier, and had been closed with several stitches, which showed as small pink beads surrounding a pink zigzag that was still slightly tender when I touched it.

"There's got to be an easier way to make a living," Peter said, shaking his head. One corner of his mouth turned up in the beginning of a smile.

"It's usually a quiet job," I said. "There's a lot of research and paperwork, a lot of waiting for people to come out of or go into one place or another. A lot of asking questions and not getting the right answers."

"And just occasionally someone tries to kill you."

"Well, that was a first," I admitted.

"What's killing *me* is waiting around for something to break," said Peter. "I don't mean I'm impatient with the way you're doing things, but I feel so powerless. I want to help you."

"You are helping me. Without the information I've gotten from you and Nora and the others, I'd be starting totally from zero."

"No, I mean I want to *really* help you." He leaned forward. "I want to be a real part of the investigation. I want to do something besides sit at home and drink too much. You could tell me what you want done. I can follow orders and I promise not to fuck anything up, and who knows—you might need someone to get in the way of a gun butt."

I thought about what he said for a moment while his eyes searched mine for encouragement. When you work out of an investigative agency, there's a lot of teamwork involved. Someone's always around to pull stakeout duty on a tough case or do legwork when you can't be in two places at once. Even in a small operation like Jake Baronian's, there was Jake and me and for the past few weeks there was Terrie, the office assistant whose fantasy of being a private eye had led her to answer Jake's latest ad, and there was the occasional hungry college student who could be hired by the job when things got busy.

I also remembered that the last time I'd been far from home and taken on an amateur assistant it had turned out rather well.

I'd felt uncomfortable about bringing an inexperienced person into the investigation, but the clock was ticking and I needed someone's help. My friend Andy had uncovered vital information I might not have been able to get my hands on, and helped break the case. Maybe this situation called for help, too.

On one hand, it could be argued that Peter was much too close to the events of the case to be an effective hired hand. On the other, no one had more at stake in the outcome than Peter did—except for Nora, of course, and she had her boys and the bookstore to think about. Peter knew everyone in town, knew the streets and roads. . . .

"Okay." I gave up trying to reason out all sides of the argument and leaped to a decision. "You've got a job. Two jobs. Your main job is to get people to talk to me. The other is to drive me around this place so I don't get hopelessly lost and they have to send Saint Bernards out to find me."

"Bloodhounds," said Peter, his face breaking into the first smile I'd ever seen on it. "It would be bloodhounds."

CHAPTER 8

A DOG HOWLED. A CAT HISSED. A TINY OLD WOMAN HELD UP
a bird cage and whistled at its occupant, who was concealed
under a flowered plastic cover. The front door to the Cedars
Veterinary Hospital banged open and a rottweiler pulled its
owner inside and stood up with his front paws on the counter,
its tongue hanging out. The woman behind the counter opened
a jar of pet vitamins and popped one into the huge mouth. The
dog stood down and chomped happily. This was obviously
a familiar routine. I wished I looked forward to visiting my
doctor as much.

"Dr. Terrell will be right with you, Mr. McKay," the woman
said to Peter. Peter found a seat next to a woman with a litter
of puppies in a cardboard box, and picked up an outdated
magazine. I walked around the outer perimeter of the office
looking at the amateurish animal paintings that some local
artist had probably traded for veterinary services. The painting
techniques were barely competent, and the artist had neglected
to learn how to draw before he or she took up a paintbrush—
the animals were pathetically out of proportion. I decided that
whatever the trade had been, the painter had almost certainly
got the better of the deal.

The door to the hallway opened and a middle-aged black
man in glasses, a white lab coat, and stethoscope walked
through into the office area. I remembered seeing him at the

funeral. He caught sight of Peter. "Peter. Good to see you. Who are we seeing today, Grumpy or Dopey?"

Peter put down the magazine and got up. "Neither one this time. Except for being old and fat, they're in perfect health."

"You're keeping them on the diet, aren't you?" The doctor's brow wrinkled with concern. "Both those boys were at least six or seven pounds overweight the last time I saw them."

I abandoned my art critique and walked over to join them. "Gordon, this is Caley Burke, an investigator from up north," said Peter. "She's here to look into what happened to Cass. Caley, this is Dr. Gordon Terrell."

"Pleased to meet you, Ms. Burke." Gordon Terrell shook my hand, then pointed to a door to our right. "Let's talk in my office."

Dr. Terrell poured us cups of coffee in thick mugs with dog and cat portraits on the sides, then sat back in his chair. "Peter, I hope you're not getting in over your head with these A.R.C. assholes. Begging your pardon, Ms. Burke."

"No pardon required, Dr. Terrell. I'm in complete agreement with you."

He smiled. "Just 'Gordon,' please. What exactly do you think happened to Cass?"

"I'm looking into the possibility that her death wasn't accidental."

Gordon sat forward and frowned. "Not accidental? Do you really think she could have been murdered?"

"There's no hard evidence yet, but until I've checked out some perfectly reasonable suspicions, I wouldn't be willing to say it didn't happen."

"Peter, what do you think? Did those white-sheeted sons of bitches actually kill her? You don't have to convince me those kind of people are capable of murder," he said. "I didn't get this black from sunbathing, and I know a thing or two about white supremacists and how they operate." He took off his glasses and rubbed his eyes. "But here? Where we live?"

"Believe me, I know," said Peter. "I want to get to the bottom of this more than anyone. And you can help."

"I'll do anything I can. You know that."

"I do know. You hung in the fight to the end—long after anyone else would have pulled out. Caley's going to need to talk to everyone who had any kind of run-in with the Andrew Weiss crowd, and you had a pretty definite one."

Gordon swiveled his chair in my direction. "You be careful about messing with these kind of people," he said. "They're criminals, and they don't much care who they hurt."

"I'm very cautious about that sort of thing these days," I assured him. My hand went up to touch the most recent scar. "I'll be extremely careful."

"I know some of them jumped you right outside the hospital soon after you joined up with the gang," Peter said. "Can you tell Caley what happened?"

"Sure." Gordon folded his glasses and closed his eyes for a moment. "Let's see, it was a Friday night. I had closed up and sent the techs and office assistants home hours before, and stayed around to catch up on some paperwork. The kids were on a camping trip with friends, so I wasn't in any particular hurry to get home." He got up, put his glasses back on, and raised the blinds on the window that looked out on the parking lot.

"It was real dark under those trees where I park my car." He pointed to a blue minivan parked in the dirt and gravel lot under a fir tree. "Nobody ever locks their cars around here, and I'd finally gotten out of the habit—it takes you a while, coming here from the city.

"So I opened the side door and a guy jumped out of the back and tackled me. There were two of them in there and two or three more under the tree. I went down, and they got in a few licks with some axe handles or something like that they were carrying, but I fought my way back up again.

"They were hitting me and shouting at me—the kind of things those people say—I don't know if they would have killed me, but at the time I wasn't making that distinction. I'd been carrying a gun ever since the first nasty phone call, and I'd been picking the kids up from school, making sure they stuck close to home. You can imagine how popular that was with them." He chuckled slightly.

I didn't have any children, but I knew a lot of teenagers. I nodded.

"So I pulled out this gun and pointed it at the nearest one and told him I'd blow his fucking head off if any one of them moved. He started screaming at them to back off, and they did."

"Did you get a good look at any of them?"

"Well, we did get real up-close and personal for a minute there," said Gordon, "but they had those goddamned hoods on. Not robes or anything, but those hoods. They could've been anybody."

"And there were five of them?" I asked him.

"Four or five. Once they saw the gun, they didn't stand still long enough for me to count them. Oh, yeah, one of them was a real little guy, not any taller than you. He mostly hung back, called me names, and egged the others on."

"What was his voice like?"

"Little. Like him. High-pitched."

I made a note to that effect in my book. "I've also heard your children have been targets of racial slurs at school."

Gordon nodded slowly, his eyes sorrowful behind the glasses. "I don't worry for myself, Ms. Burke, but I moved here and bought this practice to give my kids a better life than we had in L.A. Now, I'll admit a lot of the kids in the high school couldn't care less what color Robert and Carolyn are, and a lot more are getting used to the idea, but the A.R.C. is alive and well somewhere at that school, and my children are its targets."

"Do you think it would be any different if you hadn't gotten into Cass's fight?"

"It was my fight too, Ms. Burke. I know that taking a stand with Cass and the gang made things worse, and I'd understand if the kids didn't want me to keep on, but they're behind me."

"I'd like to talk to your son and daughter, if that's all right with you," I said. "I could come by your house, or we could meet somewhere in town."

"It might be better if you came by," Gordon said. He wrote his home address and phone number on the back of a business card and handed it across the desk. "Peter knows where this is. Would this evening be okay? The kids are going to a friend's house for supper, but they'll be back by eight. Why don't you come by then?"

Gordon walked us to the front door and opened it for us. He put a hand on Peter's shoulder. "Whatever happens, Peter," he said, "no matter how bad it gets, we can't let those bastards win."

Peter and I walked out into the dappled shade cast by the huge cedar trees that surrounded the hospital. I looked out across the lot to where Gordon's van was parked, and I was willing to bet the doors were locked now.

I'm as prone to white liberal guilt as the next white liberal, but the feeling I had right then went way beyond anything I'd experienced from reading secondhand about discrimination and bigotry. Gordon Terrell had been physically attacked because he was black, Danny Abrahams because he was a Jew or gay or both. Neither man could ever walk down a darkened street again without wondering if someone was waiting in the shadows to punish them for what they were. The possibility of senseless violence was always just around the corner.

Something was terribly wrong in this country, and I wasn't going to be able to change it or make any tremendous difference in it by any action I took now or for the rest of my life, but with this investigation maybe I could at least make a difference in Cedar Ridge.

CHAPTER 9

* * * * * * * * * * * * * * * * * *

"WHO'S NEXT?" PETER ASKED AS WE WAITED TO PULL OUT onto the highway. A steady stream of cars and RV's stretched across two lanes as far as the eye could see.

"I'd like to get the newspaper articles that covered the A.R.C. demonstrations and any other related stuff, like the vandalism against people in the gang. And of course, the accident."

"Let's go by and see Tim Wynand, then." Peter found an opening and filled it with the Chevrolet.

"Hey, that's the second one of those bumper stickers I've seen today," I told Peter, pointing at the red, white, and blue rectangle on the bumper of the car in front of us. The lettering read: "Bring Back America!"

"That's Andrew Weiss's slogan. He ends every one of his hate essays with it. It's actually kind of handy that so many people like to sport those—it helps you know who you're fighting."

"Except for the ones who don't advertise," I observed.

"Yeah," Peter said. "Except for the anonymous, invisible ones. And those are the ones who scare me the most."

We drove south on Highway 49 at a snail's pace. "Is traffic always this bad?" I asked Peter.

"Only on weekdays. From Friday noon to Sunday night it's about three times this bad." He glanced in the rearview mirror.

"You know there was a sheriff's car waiting at the corner when we pulled out from Gordon's office?"

Watching for a tail isn't easy when you're a passenger, and I hadn't mentioned the possibility to Peter, so I was grateful for his alertness. "Where is it now?"

"Two cars behind us."

"That's probably not unusual," I said hopefully.

"No. Guess I'm just paranoid."

"Probably," I agreed. "Let's turn off somewhere and see what happens."

"Okay," said Peter. "I'll take a back way to the newspaper office."

I readjusted the passenger mirror to get a view behind me. We turned on a side street and the car directly behind us continued down the highway, but the white sheriff's sedan made the turn. "Can you tell who's driving?" I asked Peter.

"Too far away."

"Slow down and let them catch up a little."

The gap between us and the sheriff's car narrowed a bit as Peter took his foot off the gas and the car slowed. He looked up into the mirror again. "Looks like Judy Roy," he said. We made another turn and Judy Roy stayed right with us, but when we pulled into the parking area of the *Foothills Sentinel*, she drove by and turned back onto the highway.

I've tailed a few people in my life, and there are techniques one uses in order to be less than obvious. True, subtlety is somewhat moot when you're driving a marked car with red and white lights on top, but all in all, Judy Roy was either a total flop in the surveillance department, or she wanted us to see her. I wondered which was the case.

The *Foothills Sentinel* served Cedar Ridge and half a dozen other small communities in the same neck of the woods, with editions on Monday and Thursday. Before Tim Wynand bought the paper, Peter told me, it mainly covered bake sales and 4-H shows. Tim had turned it into a real paper with real news.

"What's his political slant?" I asked.

"He doesn't seem to have one. He prints letters from all points on the spectrum, but his editorials usually have to do with community service issues—stuff like that. I've never known him to jump on one side or another of the fence. Tim likes to say he's not dealing in politics at the *Sentinel*, he's dealing in information."

We stepped into the welcome coolness of the *Sentinel*'s reception area, where a grandmotherly receptionist greeted us with a smile. "Hello, Mr. McKay. Is there something I can do for you?"

"We need to get a look at some back issues, Amanda," Peter told her.

"Well, I'm sure I can round up someone to show you whatever it is you need," Amanda said, glancing around.

Tim Wynand stepped out from his office. "I'll take care of these folks, Amanda. Thanks." He flashed a smile at the receptionist and waved us in.

Amanda wriggled like a happy puppy at Tim's attention. "I just love that man," she whispered to me.

"I can see why," I told her. Tim's boyish good looks could scarcely go unnoticed by any healthy heterosexual female, and his charm seemed unstudied and totally unself-conscious. I imagined a lot of women had crushes on him, and he'd probably be awfully surprised to hear it.

"What can I do for you?" Tim asked us when we had settled into his big overstuffed guest chairs and he had sent an assistant for cold drinks.

"We need to look at some back issues," I told him. "Starting with the coverage of the first A.R.C. demonstration a few months ago."

Tim nodded. "I'm sure that can be arranged." He pressed a button on the phone set and talked to someone on the other end about rounding up the papers we needed.

"We don't have the most recent stuff on microfiche yet, but we can get the appropriate issues in here and find what you're looking for." He glanced back and forth between Peter and me, curious.

"It didn't seem appropriate to bring it up yesterday," I said. "I *am* a friend of the family, but I'm also a private investigator. I came here from out of town at Nora and Peter's request, and I'm looking into the events surrounding Cass's death."

"We believe Cass was murdered, Tim," said Peter.

Tim leaned forward, his face gone white. "Murdered? God. I don't want to believe that."

"We don't have any proof yet," I hastened to point out. "What we do have are suspicions that deserve to be explored a lot further."

"Cass received death threats before the accident," Peter said, "and you know she'd driven that road a thousand times. Why would she lose control of her car on a dry road with no other car involved? There's no evidence of a blowout or brake failure . . ."

"Peter, I don't know what to say. Murder sounds so . . . I don't want to say 'farfetched.' I guess what I mean is unrealistic. We're not talking organized crime, here. Do you really believe in some sort of . . . I don't know . . . conspiracy?"

"When you put it in those terms, it sounds like we're crazy even to be talking about it, but yes, that's what we believe."

"Well, I know you're not crazy, Peter, and neither is Nora," Tim said. "And no one knows better than you know how much Cass meant to me. Just tell me what I can do to help."

A few minutes later a short stack of newspapers appeared in the arms of a young man in a *Foothills Sentinel* T-shirt.

"Thanks, Rod," Tim said. "Would you put them on the worktable over there?"

The young man deposited the stack of papers on the table and we opened them up and found the articles. "Would you like photocopies?" Tim offered. "They'd be easier to carry around." He rearranged the papers with the articles on top. "Rod, run a couple copies each of these articles, will you?" he said, handing the papers back.

"Sure thing, Mr. Wynand," said Rod, and hurried off.

"If you really want to help," I told Tim, "you could have someone on your staff research the press service archives for any mention of the A.R.C. We need to find out who these guys are and how they operate. Also anything on Andrew Weiss."

"I've got a modem at home—I'll do the search myself," Tim said. "And I'll start on it tonight. And if there's anything else—anything at all—call me."

He walked us out to the reception area, where he was the recipient of another adoring look from Amanda, which he seemed not to notice.

"Thanks, Tim," said Peter. "I wouldn't expect you to help for my sake, after . . ."

"That's all in the past, Peter. We're on the same side now. Cass's side."

"If you don't mind my asking," I said when we were back in the car, "what was that all about between you and Tim?"

Peter sighed. "Cass and Tim had a thing going before I came to town. It was pretty serious for a while, but he was married at the time, and in the end Cass called it off. It was all over and done with six months or so before she and I got serious about each other, but about the time Cass and I were deciding we wanted to be together, Tim and his wife separated, and he made a last-ditch attempt to get Cass back."

"Which failed."

"Yeah. He's never acted angry or bitter about it, but we weren't all the best of friends, either." He shifted into reverse and backed out of the parking space. "I don't know how Tim Wynand really felt about losing Cass to me, and I'm not sure how he feels about it now, but I know how I'd have felt if it had gone the other way," he said, darkness clouding his face. "I'd have wanted to kill someone."

CHAPTER 10

IT WAS ONLY MID-AFTERNOON WHEN WE LEFT THE *SENTINEL*
but I was totally burnt out. Peter suggested a cold drink and
we stopped at the Coffee Pot. Tom Flanders was at our table
with pitchers of iced tea and water, waving off the waitress.
"You folks want anything to eat?" he inquired.

I shook my head. "Too hot to eat. A couple of gallons of
liquid ought to fix me up, though. I'll have some of that tea.
You can leave the pitcher."

"Pour me one of those, too, Tom," said Peter. "I came to
Cedar Ridge from San Francisco of my own free will, but I
swear I'll never get used to the heat."

"I'll tell you," said Tom, pouring our tea, "I could charge
ten bucks a glass for this stuff and still clean up from June
to September. These foothills are so dry they suck the wet
right out of you." He sat down at the table. "So how's the
investigating?"

"Oh, we've just gotten started," I told him. "Nothing much
to report yet. I've talked to a few people around town and
gotten a few leads."

"Is that so? Well, I hope you'll keep me posted. I'm a
part of this fight too, you know. You two enjoy your drinks
and let me know if you need anything else." He left the
pitcher of tea on the table and walked back to the kitch-
en.

I drank two glasses of tea before I felt normal again. "I suppose we ought to check in with Nora and let her know how it's going," I suggested. "We're not supposed to be at Gordon's place until eight, but I'm too tired to think right now. Would you mind terribly if we stopped by the bookstore and then went home?"

"I've got a better idea," said Peter. "Just drop me at the bookstore and go back to the house and take it easy for a while. I'll give Nora a brief rundown and we'll all talk at length later tonight. We'll come back into town and have dinner at Chiang's Garden."

I was too exhausted to protest the offer of a few hours off the case, and Chinese food sounded wonderful. I followed Peter to the cashier's station, where the blond woman I had seen this morning rang up the ticket.

"How's everything, Kay?" Peter asked her.

"Oh, just fine, Peter," she said. She tried a smile, but it faded before it reached her eyes. "Same as always."

"Is that Tom Flanders's wife?" I asked Peter when we had stepped through the door into the restaurant's foyer.

"I should have introduced you," Peter said. "Forgive my lousy manners."

"That's all right. I was just curious. He's such a sociable kind of guy and she seems so withdrawn."

"Opposites attract, and all that," said Peter. "Maybe Tom didn't want a wife who'd compete with him in the meeting and greeting business."

Kay Flanders certainly wasn't likely to outshine Tom socially or in any other way, I thought, feeling strangely sorry for a woman I didn't know and probably never would. She was just a pale shadow of a woman who didn't seem to want to be noticed. She was the kind of person I might have become, with my natural bent for introversion.

Fortunately for me, other tendencies in my personality had won out. Instead of being a loner with no friends, a mundane life, and no prospects, I was a loner with a handful of friends and a job as a professional snoop that occasionally got more eventful than was good for my mental health. I decided self-congratulation might not be in order, after all.

We walked out of the air-conditioned restaurant into the blinding heat of the afternoon and I made a mental note to buy some sunglasses. I was so spaced, I almost missed seeing Deputy Judy Roy sitting in her sedan at the other end of the Coffee Pot's parking lot.

"It's nice to know somebody's looking out for us," I said.

Peter nodded. "Makes me feel real secure."

We turned out onto the highway, and two cars later the conspicuous white car edged in behind us. It stayed behind us all through town until we turned into the parking lot of the bookstore. As we slowed down to make the turn, Deputy Roy passed us on the right and turned to look at me for a fraction of second before driving on.

"What's going on here?" Peter wondered.

"It's a small town," I said. "Would you buy coincidence?"

"Not even if they were giving it away."

It was cool and dark in the house. Nora had closed the curtains on the sunward side of the house and turned on the air conditioning before we left for breakfast. I glanced in the mirror above the hallway table and frowned at the image. Even the short walk in from the driveway had turned my face red, with orange freckles standing out on my nose like caution lights. My hair was a mess. The sides were plastered down with sweat and the top stood up in spikes. Hopeless.

The red light on the answering machine was blinking; it was a message from Jake Baronian: "Burke, that painter character from down south called for you. He sounded real disappointed when I said you'd gone out of town. He left his phone number, but I've got a hunch you already have it memorized. I gave him this number, so you'll probably hear from him. Call me if you need anything. We miss you. Hurry home."

Jake was my boss, my mentor, and my friend. He'd taken a shy divorcée with an almost total lack of self-confidence and turned her into a professional investigator in only three years. I owed him my life, but he refused to acknowledge the debt. Hearing from him made me terribly homesick, so I picked up the phone and dialed his number, hoping I'd feel better after I talked to him.

"How are things in the foothills, Burke?" Jake wanted to know.

"Hot. How are things in the valley?"

"*Miserably* hot. It's good to know you're not any more comfortable than we are, at least. The air conditioning's broke and there's some guy crawling around the ducts and scaring the theater patrons downstairs."

The offices of Baronian Investigations were situated above a four-screen movie complex that had formerly been a beautiful old depression-era theater in downtown Cascade. Jake's office and mine were on either side of a huge vertical neon sign that flashed and crackled curlicues of pink and green light through the windows in the evening. If things were quiet upstairs, you could hear the sound of four films playing simultaneously in the background, very low. It was something like having a crowd of people waiting in another room, talking, and occasionally someone fired a gun or took off in a spaceship. I'd grown to love it, and besides, the box office cashiers always let us into the movies for free.

"How's Terrie?" I asked. Jake's new office assistant had only been on the job a few weeks, but she'd already become part of the family.

"Remind me never again to hire an energetic young woman who wants to become a detective."

"Too late for that on a couple of counts, Jake."

"Terrie is a wonder, but my next office assistant is going to be at least sixty-seven. Blue hair. Rheumatism. Maybe I'll hire my mother. Enough about my troubles—how's the case going?"

"Not much to go on so far. Some people are having their lives made miserable by a bunch of ignorant racists who may or may not be responsible for killing my mother's old friend. Some people are acting suspicious, some are even following me around. Nobody's shooting at me yet, and I don't have any hot prospects."

"It's not necessary to be shot at to get hot prospects. Maybe I should have told you this before."

"Wait," I said. "Let me write this down. No one has to shoot me. That's good. Any more valuable advice?"

"No, I think that ought to do it. Try and stay out of trouble this time, and hurry back. I've got Terrie doing background checks, and if you don't get home by next week I'll probably have her out on surveillance."

"Anything but surveillance, Jake. If she dies of boredom, you'll be looking for a new assistant sooner than you figured."

"Maybe you're right. Have I ever admitted you were right before?"

"Once or twice," I allowed. "I should be home by the first of next week, and I promise I won't go anywhere but the bathroom for the rest of the year. I'm sick of strange towns."

"I'm recording this conversation, you know," Jake said. "I'll play it back for you next time you get a notion to go out of town for a few days."

"I hope you do. I miss you and I miss my office, and I keep seeing my apartment gathering dust, and I just want to come home."

"I'll be right here when you do."

"Thanks, Jake. Bye."

I sat with the phone in my lap for a few minutes, aware that I had done nothing to lift my mood by calling Jake. I wanted to get in my car and drive north worse than ever, but there was still so much to be done here. I decided to lie down in the coolness of my upstairs bedroom and let some of the uneasiness and exhaustion I felt drain out of me. First, though, I'd call David. Jake was right, of course—I had the number memorized.

"David is delivering paintings to the gallery," said his grandfather's voice. "Caley?"

"Yes, Mr. Garza. David tried to call me at work, but I'm out of town right now."

"No one is threatening you with a gun?"

"Not right at the moment. Will you tell him I called?"

"I will tell him. Does he have your telephone number?"

"He does. Thanks." Well, there went my chance to feel better. After talking to Tony Garza for a few minutes, I trudged up the stairs with a glass of ice water, hoping a nap would make me feel like facing the rest of the day.

CHAPTER 11

WHEN THE PHONE RANG AGAIN, IT WAS NEARLY SEVEN o'clock. My nap long over, I'd been browsing through Cass's library. People who own bookstores are prone to being their own best customers, and Cass Lowry had not been an exception. Every possible foot of wall space, including stairwells and hallways, were covered with bookshelves. This would be a terrific place to be in a thermonuclear attack, I thought—no shortage of great insulation, not to mention reading material for those long, nuclear winter nights.

I picked up the phone. Peter was calling from town. "You know where Chiang's Garden is?"

"Pretty nearly." I had passed the green restaurant with the red pagoda-shaped roof several times in my travels, and knew I could find it again with no problem.

"Want to meet Nora and the boys and me there in about fifteen minutes?" he asked. "I'll call Gordon and tell him we might be a few minutes late."

"Fifteen minutes. I'll be there." I had already showered and changed clothes in anticipation of dinner. I grabbed my car keys and left the house.

The sun was still up, of course, but going low and golden against the treetops. Shadows stood out in sharp relief, and the distant hills, a thousand feet higher up, were a startling green-gold where the sun hit them, and deep blue in the creases. When I squinted I could see how it would look as a watercolor, and sighed when I remembered I wasn't here to find landscape-painting opportunities.

Peter and Nora and the twins were sitting at a table by the window when I entered the restaurant. There was a cold Tsingtao waiting for me and I drank it with appreciation. Matt and Harry amused themselves drawing pictures on the paper placemats. They were mostly silent, I noticed, and Nora seemed to notice it, too.

"It's going to take time for all of us to be ourselves again," she said, looking at them sadly. "If we ever can."

A pretty Asian woman about my age came to the table to take our order. I remembered seeing her with an Asian man at the funeral. They had not joined the buffet crowd at the bookstore. Nora introduced her as Patty Chiang, who owned Chiang's Garden along with her husband, Martin.

"Martin is head cook tonight," Patty said. "Our regular cook hit a cow in the road on the way up from Sacramento this afternoon and wrecked his car."

"Don't order the beef," Peter warned me in a stage whisper. Patty grabbed his menu and slapped him on top of the head with it. "No bad jokes, Peter," she said, mock-serious. "He's always like this," she told me. "You can't take him anywhere." She took our order without benefit of an order pad, and called it back in Chinese through the kitchen window.

As we ate an excellent meal of Szechuan and Hunan dishes, I remembered what Dolores had said about the Chiangs, and the locals who were staying away from the restaurant to protest their involvement with Cass's gang. All the businesses that supported Cass and opposed the A.R.C. were suffering to some extent, I supposed.

Fortunately, not everyone in town thought Andrew Weiss had the right idea about America—several local families seemed to be here tonight, as well as a couple of dozen tourists. American Rescue Coalition supporters didn't—couldn't—make up the majority of people in this community.

If Cass was killed because she frightened the A.R.C., and if that fact became public, the rest of the community would have to stand up against Andrew Weiss's brand of thinking. If that could be made to happen, maybe the soul of Cass's town wouldn't be in jeopardy after all. I could only hope.

Gordon Terrell and his teenage children lived halfway between Cedar Ridge and Hollis Creek, the next town to the north. Nora took the boys home, and Peter and I took my car north out of Cedar Ridge.

The drive up took us onto Black Mountain Road going east, and past the spot where Cass had died. I didn't recognize the location, but I saw the newly repaired guardrail and I saw Peter look over and look back, stricken. How many times would he have to drive past this place in a lifetime if he stayed in Cedar Ridge?

I glanced over at him. Tears were spilling from his eyes and he wiped at them angrily with the back of his hand.

"I have some tissues in the glove compartment," I said.

"Thanks." Peter opened the glove box. "That's not all you've got in there," he commented. He reached around the Walther and found the packet of facial tissues next to it.

"I've been trying to forget about that damned thing since I put it in there," I said. "Hope it didn't alarm you."

"I've seen them before," he said, closing the little door. "But I don't like them much."

I didn't either.

From the time I'd first gone to work for Jake Baronian, the Walther had been my constant companion. It had been Jake's gun originally, given to me when I started training, and carried as a condition of employment. From a position of fear and ignorance about firearms, I had come to respect their power and accept the responsibility of owning and carrying one.

In almost any other job, I would never have felt the need to go armed, but Jake had experienced some close calls in his career, and wanted me to have an edge should it ever be needed. It had only been needed once, so far, and it was the memory of that incident that had damaged my previously friendly relationship with my pistol.

Gordon's place was a two-story log house on fifteen acres of mixed oaks and softwoods a mile from the main road along a one-lane dirt track that covered my car in a thick coating of yellow-brown dust. Peter pointed out the driveway hidden in among trees and rocks, and I turned in and continued another quarter mile up a steep hill to the house.

When we pulled up in front of Gordon's door, I took the gun out of the glove compartment and zipped it up in a duffel bag in the trunk—the one that I used to carry to the pistol range. I locked the trunk with a sigh of relief. The next time I looked at the Walther it would be because I wanted to; I just had no idea when that might be.

Land and houses were cheap here compared to Los Angeles or San Francisco, which made the area popular with retired people and those with an outside source of income like Peter and Danny. Peter's income has derived from book illustration and occasional cover paintings. Like a lot of people in his line of work, he didn't live in New York but dealt with publishers by mail. Danny earned his money from writing, mainly for newspapers and magazines, though Peter had also mentioned that he was writing a book about Elias.

Other immigrants like Dolores and Gordon found business opportunities in the community. After the accident that put her in the wheelchair, Dolores had moved to Cedar Ridge with a truckload of antiques and opened the Antique Barn. Gordon had bought a small animal practice from the widow of a deceased veterinarian and brought his two children from Los Angeles not long after his wife died.

"Mary had family in L.A. and she liked it there," said Gordon as he showed us around the house. "I came from Wisconsin, originally. I loved the woods and the idea of having some space around me." We walked up a wide stairway and into a library area overlooking the room below. Two leather chairs flanked a reading table piled high with books.

"The kids agreed to try living here for two years," Gordon continued. "Robert will graduate this year, and Carolyn the year after that, so it'll be up to them what they want to do and where they want to live. They've been pretty good about adjusting, all things considered."

"Hey, Papa!" a young woman's voice called from downstairs. "We brought Mark with us, okay?"

"Of course it's okay," Gordon called down over the upstairs railing. "I asked you to bring him, didn't I?" He turned back to us. "Mark's a friend of theirs from school. He told Robert a story I think you'll want to hear."

We went back downstairs into the spacious living room where three teenagers pored over a stack of CD's in front of a wall of stereo components. Robert and a boy with blond, waist-length hair sported heavy-metal T-shirts and jeans. Carolyn wore an African print skirt and blouse.

"No Megadeth on the downstairs stereo," Gordon warned them as we crossed the living room. "That's why I sound-proofed the extra bedroom."

"We're just picking some stuff out for later, Dad," said Robert.

"Well, come meet our guests and let's talk a bit first," Gordon suggested. "This is Robert and Carolyn, and this is their friend Mark Birdsall. You guys all know Peter McKay, and this is Caley Burke. She's in town looking into the A.R.C."

"*Those* assholes!" Mark Birdsall said, shaking his head.

"Mark actually met up with some of those guys," said Robert.

"He saw their headquarters or something," added Carolyn.

"Let's let Mark tell his own story," said Gordon. "We've heard this before, Mark, but I'd like you to tell Caley what you told us."

"Okay." Mark shifted on the couch to face me. I opened my notebook and took out a pen.

"Well, to begin with, it was Saturday night, and I was partying with three other guys from school."

"How long ago was this?"

"About a month ago. There was this other guy with us who was legal, so he loaded us in the back of his truck, bought a couple cases of beer, and we started driving around."

They had gone to several houses in the area, picking up friends of the man Mark identified as Dale Reid, the driver of the truck. Toward the end of the ride, Mark had ended up sitting with his back against the tailgate so he could see where the truck was going.

They headed northeast from Cedar Ridge toward Black Mountain and drove up a winding road into the hills, finally pulling up at a small frame house with half a dozen rusted-out car bodies in the yard and a pair of emaciated pit bulls chained inside a kennel attached to the side of the house.

"It was real dark in the house—almost no lights on at all in the place—so I was sitting down with a beer before I noticed the walls."

"What about them?"

"You couldn't see them for one thing. All you could see were these posters and shit. A lot of Nazi stuff and a lot of, I don't know, KKK kind of stuff and all these bumper stickers pasted up that said: 'Bring Back America!' "

Peter looked at me. I nodded and kept writing.

"It was totally creepy," Mark went on. "I was like, 'Let's get out of here' to the guys I was with, and then this Dale Reid guy that had driven us there got up and started talking to us like we were there for a meeting or something."

"What kind of things did he say?"

"I didn't stick around for a lot of it, but he started out about how America was founded by whites for whites and it was a white culture and a white nation, and we'd forgotten that and started letting blacks and Jews and whoever else run the country"—he paused for an apologetic look at Robert and Carolyn—"and about how we had to take back what was ours and shit like that.

"He was giving me the major creeps. I mean, I'd just gone along for some beers, and here I was getting this total political lecture. I got two of my friends out of there and we left. We couldn't get anyone to drive us, so we walked back to town."

"One of your friends stayed?"

"I don't know if I'd call him a friend. It was Ken Woodworth. He was the one who had the idea of partying with Dale Reid in the first place. He acted like he *liked* those guys. He wouldn't leave, so we went without him.

"Ken Woodworth—shit." Mark shook his head and looked down at the carpet. "I see him at school now, and he's all, 'You're a coward, Birdsall! You're a race traitor!' and other stuff I'm not going to repeat, but I don't give a shit." He looked up at me. "I wasn't raised to think like that."

"Do you think you could find this place again?" Peter asked.

"I might have to ride around a few of those roads, but I'd find it sooner or later if I looked. I just never wanted to look, you know?"

"I know. But we might need to find the place sometime. Would you help us if we needed you?"

Mark looked at his friends, then back at Peter, and nodded. "Sure. I'd help."

CHAPTER 12

WHEN I GOT BACK TO THE HOUSE THERE WAS ANOTHER MESsage, this time from David, saying that he had to go to Los Angeles for two days and he'd call as soon as he got back. After everyone else had gone upstairs I played it again, just to hear David's voice, and fought back tears of loneliness.

David seemed so far away from me and the things I was experiencing right now that I had to admit Nora had a point. It would be impossible to have any kind of real relationship with someone who lived most of the length of California away. I went upstairs and read the letters he'd written me since I left him down south. In my present emotional state, the letters seemed as significant for the things they didn't say as for the things they did, and reading them only made me cry.

As long as I felt like shit anyway, I decided I might as well start in on the Andrew Weiss book. It seemed important to me to know as much as possible about the mindset that threatened Cedar Ridge and a lot of other formerly peaceful places around the country.

Cass had read the book after the first A.R.C. demonstration and asked the other gang members to read it, too. She had refused to buy more than one copy for fear of putting any more money than absolutely necessary into Andrew Weiss's pocket. This one shabby copy had been passed from hand to hand, educating the members of the gang as to just what they were up against. Margin notes in various handwriting styles proclaimed various negative opinions: "This dog needs a muzzle!" "What a psycho!"

I turned the first page and started in. Three hours later I was finished, still propped up on the bed, eyes glazed over. Andrew Weiss's approach to curing America of the curse of interracial cooperation and multiculturalism was presented in a calm and reasoning style, calling on Mom, family values, and Old Glory in ways so subtle the reader would almost feel crazy not to agree. There were touches of self-effacing humor to lighten things up, and an aura of quiet charisma that was downright frightening. If this guy ever decided to take to the airwaves, and if he wasn't ugly as an Edsel, he could probably be elected to public office.

The last page of the book was an advertisement for another Andrew Weiss book and a whole passel of political pamphlets available by mail order from an address in the Los Angeles area. "No thanks, no way," I said aloud. I put the book down and got up to wash my hands.

"I went to high school with Dale Reid," Nora told me the next morning when we were sitting around the Coffee Pot waiting for breakfast.

Danny and Dolores had come along to hear the latest developments. Peter had stayed home—to work on some illustrations, he said—but I suspected it was also to have some time alone.

"He was a couple of years behind me," Nora was saying, "so I didn't know him well then, but I knew him well enough not to like him. After I married Eddie I saw a lot more of him than I wanted to."

Tom Flanders showed up with a waitress loaded down with plates, and a pot of coffee that he proceeded to pour all around. "How's the investigating going?" he asked me as he filled my cup.

"Okay so far," I told him.

The waitress set down our plates and left. Tom looked over the table. "You folks need some more cream and sugar," he said. "I'll go get you some."

I turned back to Nora. "So Dale Reid's a friend of Eddie's?"

"Eddie gravitates to guys like Dale whose IQ's are smaller than their hat sizes. Their idea of fun is to get shit-faced and find a fight. They're also bigoted and proud of it. Eddie never talked like them around me, but he'd defend them to me until I wanted to scream." She laughed. "Come to think of it, I did scream a time or two. I have to wonder now what made me stick around long enough to sink that low."

She sipped at her coffee and looked thoughtful. "I think when it came down to it, I divorced Eddie's friends as much as I did him. In fact, I've told him I don't want him taking Matt and Harry anywhere near those jerks on the weekends they're with him. He's afraid I'll keep him from seeing the boys, so he's been pretty good about it."

I watched Nora as she spoke. She didn't seem to be making the connection I was from Eddie to Dale to the A.R.C., and this didn't seem like a good time to force it on her. She'd also mentioned Johnny Hughson as one of Eddie's friends, and I got the distinct feeling Hughson was one person who wasn't happy with my involvement in this case. He and whoever he'd been talking to on the phone yesterday. Those two and just possibly Judy Roy.

I glanced at Dolores and Danny in turn and they didn't seem to get the Eddie connection, either. Well, why should they? To them, Eddie was probably just a local boy they'd known casually since they came to town. He wasn't part of their social crowd, but they didn't seem to automatically relegate him to the role of enemy, and maybe I shouldn't either.

Oh, to hell with that. It was my job to be suspicious of everybody, so I might as well stop feeling guilty about it and take some professional satisfaction from it.

"Is Eddie still working for the Forest Service?" I asked as casually as I could manage.

"Still there," said Nora. "He's a crew chief now."

Tom came back with cream and sugar and put them on the table. "You tell me if you need anything," he said. "This girl's new and she forgets sometimes." He refilled our ice water.

"Where does Dale Reid work?" I asked.

"Same place as Eddie," Nora said. "At the Cedar Ridge Forest Fire Station."

I nodded as I made a note.

Breakfast was good, just like the day before. Up in Cascade I frequently eat breakfast out at a little cafe where all the waitresses know my name and how I eat my eggs. When I'm in a strange place I sometimes have breakfast for dinner too, because it's the hardest thing to do dead wrong. The Coffee Pot had my full approval. They gave good breakfast.

Mike McCutcheon came in with a couple of guys who looked like local businessmen. He gave us a wave and sat down a few tables away. Several people in the room waved and said "Hi" to him.

"I guess Mike's a pretty popular guy around town," I commented.

"Practically a celebrity," said Dolores. "He's some kind of war hero, though that's all a long time before I came here— Vietnam. The clippings are framed on his office wall. He was awarded a Silver Star, I believe. Then he came home and took over the family business." She looked over at Mike, who was charming one of Tom's young waitresses with a smile and a wink. "His attitude toward women isn't exactly commendable, but he's a tireless booster for the interests of Cedar Ridge."

Mike caught my eye and gave me a friendly wave and a smile. I returned the wave and turned back to my coffee. I still wasn't interested in seeing his car collection.

I consulted my notebook as the waitress cleared away the plates. "Nora, I think it was you who mentioned that there was some local television coverage of the A.R.C. demonstrations."

"That's right," Nora said. "Right after the first get-together on the corner Mom called Rocky Marx, a TV reporter who works at one of the network affiliates in Sacramento. She wanted to know if this whole deal would be newsworthy down in the flatlands."

"Was it?"

"Not so much the first time. Rocky agreed to come up and do a few interviews after the fact, but she told Mom if they ever came back to call her the instant they showed up and she'd bring up a camera crew and get it on tape."

"So she called, and they came." I was beginning to get an idea that might be worth a lot to me. "And did they tape the A.R.C. guys?"

"Oh, it's better than that," said Dolores. "We told you how Cass confronted them at the demonstration? Well they got that on tape, too."

"Did any of you record it when it came on the news?"

Danny shook his head. "Rocky Marx told Cass she'd send her a tape of all the footage they took, so none of us bothered to take it off the evening news."

"And did she send the tape?" I prompted.

"Yeah, but it didn't arrive until Thursday," said Danny. "Cass had the copy in her car when . . ."

"Where is it now?" I asked.

"Nobody ever found it."

Tom shook his head sorrowfully. "This whole business is just so damned awful."

"All's not lost," I said. "The TV station will have a master of that tape. I think I'd like to get a look at it."

CHAPTER 13

PETER HAD ASKED ME TO COME AND GET HIM IF I WENT OUT investigating, but he'd looked so exhausted that morning I didn't have the heart to drag him out to face more unpleasant facts about the death of the woman he loved. He was still having trouble sleeping; I had awakened to hear him roaming the house at least four times during the previous night. It would be good for him to get back to his artwork, and he had deadlines to meet. As soon as we had finished breakfast and the others left for job or home, I made a phone call to the television station to set up a meeting, then gassed up the car and drove down through the arid foothills to Sacramento.

KSCR TV was housed in a steel-and-plaster construction that had been right out there on the architectural edge in 1959. Forty-some years later it looked just plain butt-ugly standing in the middle of an asphalt parking lot with a few pitiful trees trying to survive in concrete containers fertilized with Styrofoam coffee cups and cigarette butts.

It was even hotter, if possible, in Sacramento than it had been a couple of thousand feet higher. I could feel myself wilting as I climbed out of the car and into the heat. I counted every step—eighty-four—to the aluminum-edged glass doors and the promise of air conditioning.

"I'm here to see Rocky Marx," I told the receptionist. "She's expecting me."

Rocky Marx was like a nuclear device: small and bursting with energy. I had to rush to keep up with her as she led me through mazelike hallways to the control room. "I'm glad you called," she said over her shoulder as I hurried along behind her. "I think it's entirely too handy a coincidence that Cass Lowry died less than a week after we shot this tape. I called the Sheriff's Department and asked them to come down here and view it, but they're happy with their accidental death theory."

"Cass's family isn't," I said. "That's why they hired me."

"I feel terrible about what happened to Cass, but I loved getting this story," she said as she turned right onto another identical hallway. "It's the kind of thing that sets people right on their asses. We're so complacent about things like this in California, you know? 'It can't happen here.' 'Those kind of people live somewhere else.' Bullshit."

She made a sharp left and we entered a large room lined with electronics and unfamiliar towers of equipment. A technician watched a bank of monitors, fingers poised above a row of lighted buttons. Rocky led the way into a smaller room filled with tape decks and monitors and motioned me into a chair. "This is the three-quarter-inch master tape of the footage we got that day in Cedar Ridge," she said after closing the door. She put an oversize tape into an oversize tape deck and shuttled through some unrelated footage at the beginning. "Before you go, I'll have someone dub you a half-inch copy to take with you."

Images of people in robes and hoods began to dance on the monitor and Rocky stopped and reversed the tape to the beginning of the A.R.C. coverage. "This is everything we shot that day," she told me, zeroing in on the first image and freezing it. "We edited it and added some voiceover in the studio before we ran it on the news, but this has all the important stuff."

Rocky turned down the room light, then pressed a button and the tape began to play.

An unfocused close-up of a hooded figure resolved itself to sharpness as the videographer adjusted the focus. The figure's eyes were barely visible in the recesses of the hood. The camera pulled back to a full-body shot, showing plain leather work boots below the hem of the robe.

The camera panned right and came to rest on three children, possibly between the ages of seven and ten, anonymous in robes and hoods. Along with three adults, they walked up and down the line of cars with armfuls of leaflets and dropped them into car windows as the cars waited their turn at the four-way stop at Cedar Avenue and Highway 49. Each robe was embroidered in red, back and front, with the letters A.R.C.

The picture jumped, and a voice said: "On Rocky in five. Four. Three." Rocky Marx stood on the corner in the bright sunshine in front of the line of cars, the hooded children clearly visible behind her. "The people you see here," she began after a couple seconds of silence, "represent the American Rescue Coalition, an ultraconservative organization founded by a writer of political books and leaflets who calls himself Andrew Weiss.

"The Coalition believes that America is being ruined by multiculturalism and the growing acceptance of gays, and that the country should be in the hands of a Caucasian majority. Not everyone agrees."

The picture cut to an angry man throwing a leaflet in the face of one of the A.R.C. people, then to a woman shaking her fist at them out of her car window. There were shots of people walking with signs that read "This is a White Man's Country." "Let the Majority Rule." "Let's Bring Back America."

Rocky and a hooded man stood in front of a camera. "Five. Four. Three."

"Andrew Weiss avoids having his picture shown, or making any kind of media appearance. Exactly who is he and what is the American Rescue Coalition?" Rocky inquired of the man. She held a microphone in front of him.

"Andrew Weiss is a man who knows what's wrong with this country and how we can fix it," the man said, his words somewhat muffled by the layer of cloth over his face. "We're part of the American Rescue Coalition, and we contribute time and money to the causes that Andrew Weiss feels are important to America."

"And what *is* important to America, according to Andrew Weiss?" Rocky asked.

"To return the government of this country to the white Christian majority," said the man. "To end the domination of non-white, non-Christian special interest groups and bring America back to its true origin and destiny."

"Why is Andrew Weiss such a mystery man?" Rocky asked him. "Why doesn't anyone know what he looks like, or sounds like, for that matter?"

"Andrew Weiss isn't just one man," the hooded figure said, and I began to realize what was bothering me most about his speech: it was entirely canned, learned by rote and repeated like a mantra. "He's every guy who loves America and hates what it's become. He's every guy who sees his country falling apart at the seams and wants to do something about it. He knows what we're thinking; how we're feeling. I don't care what he looks like. I'm glad he's out there, somewhere, looking out for us."

The camera tightened the shot and centered on Rocky. "Some of the residents of Cedar Ridge aren't willing to sit back and let the American Rescue Coalition have the last word," Rocky said. "Cassandra Lowry and her group of Cedar Ridge business people have been actively opposing the influence of the A.R.C. since their first demonstration here in April of this year."

The image cut to another two-shot, this time Rocky and Cass Lowry. Cass looked much as the last time I'd seen her, healthy and fresh-faced and alive. She didn't look within ten years of her age, though her hair was shot through with silver.

"Ms. Lowry, how do you and your organization of local citizens feel about the presence of the A.R.C.?"

"We recognize their right to be here and to demonstrate," Cass said into the microphone, "but we can't in any way support their views or their actions on behalf of those views."

"You mean the passing out of Andrew Weiss literature to motorists and passers-by?"

"Yes, and the presence of children taking part in this activity. These children are being raised to believe that hate and bigotry are not only normal, but desirable. They're being poisoned."

"How are you and your group opposing the politics of the A.R.C.?" Rocky asked.

"Well, we're not here to interfere with any legal activity," said Cass. "The Constitution gives them the right to assemble peaceably, but in our opinion, they're creating a traffic hazard at this intersection, and we've asked the sheriff's deputies to make arrests on that basis."

"Have any arrests been made so far?"

"No," said Cass. "There haven't been any arrests."

The tape showed a few more shots of demonstrators and cars and curious tourists and local citizens. Some other people were interviewed about their feelings. I didn't recognize any of them except Peter, Danny, and Dolores. Nora had watched the demonstration from a nearby office with Matt and Harry. Eddie hadn't picked up the boys that weekend and she hadn't wanted them too close in case trouble broke out.

"The really good part is coming up," Rocky said. "Cass walked up to one of these bozos and we followed her with a camera and a mike. It was the same one I talked to earlier."

A few shots later, Cass was standing in front of one of the hooded demonstrators, asking him questions. "Why did you come out here with these people?" she asked him.

"Because I believe in America," the man said. Other demonstrators stood near, holding their signs but not speaking.

"I do too," Cass said, "but the America I believe in includes people of all races and religions and points of view trying to live together and get along."

"The America you believe in is a lie," said the hooded man. "This is a white man's country and a Christian country. That's how it was founded, and that's its destiny."

"You exclude women from your country, too?" Cass asked him.

"Feminist bitches like you, and lesbians and queer-loving, pro-abortion, knee-jerk liberals who're ruining this wonderful country of ours, yes."

Cass laughed. "How can you use the term knee-jerk when you're standing there quoting Andrew Weiss hate literature like it was Holy Scripture?" She turned to face one of the silent demonstrators. "And how can you justify bringing children into this? I can't believe you're so proud of what you're doing that you bring your children along to help."

"My children—" the second man began, but the first man waved him to silence.

"Those children are going to inherit the America we're giving them," he said. "They're happy and proud to be here with their parents."

"Why can't *he* answer me?" said Cass, pointing to the man who had tried to talk. "Does he need you to be his mouthpiece?"

Rocky froze the image and pointed to the monitor. "Now here's where it gets really interesting," she said. "Watch Cass Lowry carefully as she talks to this other guy."

Cass stepped closer to the other man. "If you really believe in what you're doing here, why can't you talk for yourself?" The camera had moved in to a close two-shot of Cass and the silent man. She peered into the hood, trying to meet his eyes. He turned his head, but not before I could see her expression change slightly. The silent man held his sign up in front of him like a shield and kept his head averted. Cass stepped back, away from him.

Rocky stopped the tape again. "Right there!" she said. "Did you see her face? I think she ID'd that guy." She ran the tape back and we watched it again: Cass looked into his eyes, her face changed, he looked away, she stepped back. "Do you see what I mean?"

I sat back in my chair. My shoulder muscles ached with tension from leaning forward to catch every second of the exchange. "You're right," I said. "She knew him. I'm sure of it."

Rocky ran the rest of the tape. Cass stepped back from the silent man and addressed the other one again. "I believe you're wrong," she said. "And I think most people in this country think you're wrong, too." Her voice held some new emotion that made it waver just a bit. "And I'm going to keep fighting you and people like you as long as I live." She turned her back on the man and walked away. The screen went black.

The room lights came up, reminding me of the real world outside the video monitor. I stood up, feeling a bit dizzy. "She lived a little less than six more days," said Rocky, punching the rewind button. "I know the cops don't agree, but I think these clowns killed her."

CHAPTER 14

THE ROAD FROM SACRAMENTO INTO THE GOLD COUNTRY starts out as a flat ribbon of blacktop, then rises gradually into the foothills of the Sierras. The landscape changes, becoming less barren and less polluted the further one gets from the city. Looking back down the rise in my rearview mirror, I could see a pall of gray-brown haze hanging over the valley.

I made a face. It was hard to believe I'd been breathing that shit. I love the excitement of a big city, but the immense valley between the coastal mountains and the Sierra Nevadas, where a lot of California's population and most of its agriculture is situated, is a pollution magnet. Between cars, manufacturing, and agriculture, so much toxic junk gets pumped into the air it's a wonder anyone's lungs work at all. Sacramento isn't even the worst of it, being located at one end of a river delta and getting a shot of onshore fresh air most afternoons, but it's bad enough. I was glad to be driving east and upward.

Ahead of me the road ascended through pine and scrub oak and manzanita and a hundred other plants I couldn't name. Signs announced historical markers ahead, and the markers themselves went by seconds later. I wondered if anyone but me ever stopped to look at them; I made a point of pulling over at each one I saw when I was on a leisurely trip, to put places to the events I'd read about over the years. I didn't consider this a leisurely trip, so I kept going up the hill.

Every fourth-grader in California is required to study California history, like it or not. I was one of the ones who liked it, and still do. I've lived in nine different states since I was old enough to know the difference between one place and another, but I'm a Californian at heart, and its history fascinates me. The librarians in Cascade actually call me on the phone when a new California history book comes in.

Looking out over the arid foothills, I could imagine how this countryside looked a hundred, two hundred years ago—very much as it did now except for the fences. The few towns on this stretch of road were widely separated, the land in between given over mainly to cattle ranching.

It was easy to look at this land and see Spanish soldiers leading parties of settlers and priests west from the deserts of Arizona to the San Francisco bay, or wagonloads of optimists heading for the gold fields where most of them would end up poorer than when they arrived, and a few would become millionaires overnight. The image of the promised land out where the sun sets had turned a wilderness into the most populous state in the country in just a bit over two hundred years.

Not all that much had changed in that time, it seemed—people still thought of California as some kind of fantasy world where they could escape the humdrum reality of ordinary life, and to a limited extent they were right. A lot of the state might be just as deadly dull as any other place, but there was a special feeling about it that couldn't be denied. California still thought of itself—right or wrong—as El Dorado.

The highway into the foothills from Sacramento becomes narrower and more contorted as it winds its way up the mountainsides of oaks and granite and dead grass. Every so often a passing lane appears, allowing you to get around some guy who thinks going over forty is roughly akin to playing Russian roulette with an automatic.

There had been just such a driver ahead of me for a couple of miles, an older white pickup with an amateurish paint job, that had pulled off from the side of the road in front of me, then slowed down to a snail's pace. I gassed off and saved myself a collision, but then I was forced to ride his ass just a little so as not to miss my next chance to pass him. The hills were getting steeper and the engine in the rental car didn't seem energetic enough for fast uphill getaways.

I kept looking for a good passing opportunity, but I didn't know the road ahead well enough to chance the illegal ones, and when I came to the legal ones there were always cars in the oncoming lane. Finally I saw a sign promising a passing lane ahead. When the extra lane materialized, I shifted down and gassed up, anticipating the pickup's move to the right.

He didn't move over. I pulled up behind him and flashed my lights, but he crawled along in the passing lane, unaware or uncaring. I put on my turn signal and moved into the slow lane, planning to pass him on the other side. Just as I came even with his rear bumper, he veered into that lane, causing me to take my foot off the gas and apply the brake to keep from ramming him.

Okay, so now the moron was in the slow lane where he belonged. I looked ahead on the road, and there was still plenty of passing room before the lane gave out, despite the fact that I'd lost most of my momentum. I sped up to pass him on the left, resisting the urge to look over. As I came up beside him he veered suddenly, coming over onto my side. My right window was filled with white. I pulled to the left, going into the oncoming lane.

A logging truck came around the curve ahead and blasted its horn. My heart thudded. I braked and fell back behind the white pickup. The truck roared by, peppering my windshield with scraps of bark. My ears were still ringing, and my throat had gone dry.

I looked ahead. The pickup was back in the right-hand lane and there was still some room left to pass him if he didn't decide to pull the lane-change stunt again. I stomped on the gas and zoomed ahead of him just as the lane ended, thanking the Chevy's engine for giving me all it had.

I floored it for a few miles to get well ahead of the white pickup and tried to get my breathing under control. He was probably a random highway idiot of the type the odds say you have to run up against every so often, but a recent experience with being run off the road had left me gun-shy in that department. I watched the mirrors for a while, but I didn't see him again.

I was most of the way to Cedar Ridge when I saw the revolving red and white lights behind me. I glanced down at the speedometer, fully expecting to learn I'd been doing seventy, but the needle held steady at fifty-five. I don't catch myself sticking to the speed limit all that often; I decided I must have been thinking too hard.

I slowed down to a crawl and pulled over onto the berm, throwing up a cloud of dry dirt. Behind me, the big-shouldered four-wheel drive sheriff's vehicle disgorged a big-shouldered deputy who sauntered up to my car like he was being paid by the hour. I rolled down my window and searched my handbag for my license. There's always a cop around when you *don't* need one; where was this guy when the jerk in the pickup was playing road tag with me?

"Afternoon," the deputy said when he came even with the window.

I put my head out and looked up at him. He was average height, blond, and muscular. A golden mustache adorned his upper lip. His shiny black name tag said "Bellenger." A little alarm was going off somewhere in the back of my mind.

"Hi, there, ma'am," he said as he came up to the side of the car. "How's it going today?"

I shrugged. "All right until now."

"Hot one today, isn't it? 'Course they're all hot in July." He took off his uniform cap and wiped his brow with a forearm, then set the hat on the roof of my car.

"Just out of curiosity, was I speeding?" I asked, giving him my most innocent smile. "This is a rental car, and I'm not sure the speedometer works." I tapped the glass over the instrument panel for effect. I once read an entire book on how to get off the hook when stopped for speeding, but it never seems to work for me.

Deputy Bellenger put his hands on either side of the window opening and leaned his weight against the car. "No, you weren't speeding," he said. "But this is an unsafe area in general, and there's a lot of things a person could do around here besides speeding that might end up endangering their lives." He smiled.

"Educate me," I said. I was already out of patience with this posturing, and by now I had recalled what bothered me about his name—Craig Bellenger was the deputy who had blown Cass off when she called about the A.R.C.—the one who said there were sheriff's deputies on the scene during the first A.R.C. demonstration. My relations with law enforcement have been genial, all things considered, but I was willing to make an exception for this stooge.

"Well, if I were you I'd take it real easy," he said.

"Define easy," I ventured, meeting his gaze.

His eyes gave me the creeps. He looked like he was enjoying this macho game-playing. "Well," he drawled, "I wouldn't rush into anything and I wouldn't go following anyone too close. Stunts like that can get a person hurt."

"Is that the end of the lesson?" I asked, checking the road behind me in the rearview. It was empty.

"It is if you take it serious." He leaned further into the car, inches from my face. "How serious do you take it?"

"Deadly serious, Craig," I replied. Before he could react to the familiarity, I started the engine and took off, spitting dirt and rocks all over him. I glanced in the mirror and saw him reaching into the car for his radio mike with one hand and trying to pound the dust out of his uniform with the other. His hat had flown off my roof and rolled into the far lane. A semi rolled over it with all axles.

It was one of those short-term satisfactions you know you're going to pay for later, but it felt awfully good at the time. I watched Craig Bellenger growing smaller in my side mirror and wondered if I should maintain a lower profile for a while. Being threatened by a sheriff's deputy because I was investigating a suspicious accident in his jurisdiction didn't exactly fill me with confidence.

CHAPTER 15

I WASN'T SURPRISED TO SEE DEPUTY JUDY ROY TAKE UP her unsubtle tail position on me soon after I came back into Cedar Ridge. I turned into the parking lot of the *Foothills Sentinel* and let her drive by without so much as a look of acknowledgment; I'd had a bellyful of local law enforcement bullying for one day, thank you.

"I'm here to see Mr. Wynand," I told the receptionist, and "No, he isn't expecting me," to the anticipated question.

"Oh, we don't stand much on ceremony up here in the mountains," she said with a smile, and I regretted my crankiness. I smiled back as best I could and waited for Tim to come out.

The receptionist buzzed him and he appeared a moment later. "Well, what a pleasant surprise," he said when he saw me. He opened the gate next to Amanda's desk to let me in. "Amanda, did my package from Los Angeles come today?"

"The Hollywood box? No, Mr. Wynand. No sign of it. I haven't seen the FedEx man yet today."

"You'll buzz me as soon as it gets here?"

"I certainly will," she said.

"How could I possibly run this place without you?" he asked. She blushed and lowered her eyes demurely.

Tim escorted me back to his office. "It's good to see you

again, Caley. Is it all right if I call you Caley?" he asked with a shy smile.

"Of course. There's no reason for us to be so formal, all things considered." I smiled back. Tim Wynand's boyish charm was infectious. His eyes studied me with candid interest and seemed to invite confidence. "Have you turned up anything on the A.R.C.?"

"Oh, I've got tons of stuff I downloaded from the net," he said, opening a desk drawer and bringing out a sheaf of printouts. "I called up to the house, hoping you were free to have lunch, but Peter said you'd left this morning and he didn't know where you'd gone."

"I went to Sacramento, and somewhere along the way I forgot about lunch entirely." I looked at my new Mickey Mouse watch, a present from David after my old one had been ruined in the explosion that earned me the stitches on my forehead. It was almost two and I was starving. "I'm starving," I said to Tim.

"Then let's go over these after we get some food into you," he said. He picked up the stack of paper and led the way out of the office. "Do you have a preference?"

"My local restaurant experience is limited to the Coffee Pot and Chiang's," I told him.

"Then it's time you had a new experience," he said. "We can take my car."

Tim's car was a modest blue compact, parked at the far end of the *Sentinel* parking lot in an unmarked slot. Evidently, he didn't believe in taking special privileges. I was impressed, but also damp and overheated by the time we trekked to the car and he started the engine and the air conditioner.

Summer always hits me hard, and it makes me wonder why I don't live on the coast, where it's bearable, or even in San Francisco, where they don't have a summer at all, except for three sunny weeks in September.

Tim edged into the tourist traffic and headed south on the highway. "There's a terrific Italian place on the south edge of town, run by an Australian," he said.

"Australians can't cook," I informed him. "They put beets on hamburgers."

"Well, this one can," he said. "The pasta's fresh, the sauces are terrific, and it's long on Aussie ambience. You'll love the place."

"Be still, my stomach," I sighed.

The restaurant was as wonderful as advertised, and the Australian, a bearded giant by the name of Desmond Gunn, as bluff and hearty as any Down Under tourism commercial. We were shown to a table with a fabulous view and treated like celebrities. This place, situated high on a hill overlooking a million trees, was totally unlike any part of Cedar Ridge I'd seen so far. I said as much to Desmond.

"It's almost as pretty as home," he said, "but there's no culture outside the yogurt aisle of the bloody supermarket."

"Well, maybe you'll bring us a bit, Des," said Tim.

"I'll do better than that, mate," the Aussie declared, "I'll bring you a bottle of Rosemount Shiraz-Cabernet."

"Can I afford it?"

"You can or you're a cheap son of a bitch," was the reply.

"And what are we having for lunch?" Tim asked him.

Desmond looked us over with a professional eye. "Pesto pasta with spinach and Pompeiian sausage," he said. "Nothing better than that. The only way to top a meal like that is to go home and make love all afternoon."

Tim blushed, and I didn't want to imagine the color I was probably turning myself. "Just bring us the pasta, please, Des," he said, trying not to laugh.

"You got it, mate," Desmond replied with a mock salute, and headed for the kitchen, bellowing our order at the top of his lungs while tables of people turned to stare.

"I thought I'd seen everything this town had to offer," I confessed. "I can see I was a bit too hasty in that judgment."

"Cedar Ridge is a varied place," Tim said. "People come here from all over the country, all over the world, even. They're looking for a kind of sanctuary, a life away from the disorder of the cities, the illness that infects the whole country." His blue eyes darkened a little.

"Yeah," I agreed, "this country has a lot of problems, and they're not going to go away by themselves."

"I have a sort of ideal vision of Cedar Ridge," said Tim.

"It's something I've thought about ever since I came here. I'd like to think I'll have a hand in molding it into that vision." His eyes took on a faraway look.

"Does this mean you're going into politics?" I asked.

Tim laughed, coming back to the present time and place. "I don't do politics," he said. "But I see this town as a sort of microcosm—a model of what this country should be like." He looked out over the hills through the big picture window beside our table. "A place where you can raise your kids and live your life and never worry about getting mugged or knifed in a dark alley."

"Or being killed by fanatic bigots?" I put in. "I don't mean to ruin your image of Cedar Ridge, but if you scratch this town, there are some pretty unpleasant things just under the surface."

Tim blinked. "Well, it's not perfect, I'll admit. But the notion that Cass was somehow killed by the A.R.C. is still a pretty farfetched one, no matter how fervently Peter may believe it. I mean, it sounds like something out of a TV show. This is real life, Caley. Most people don't get themselves murdered by some kind of dark conspiracy."

He pushed his wineglass aside and moved the printouts to the center of the table. "But I promised you and Peter I'd dig up what I could on these guys, and this is it. A few stories and articles I took off the information services—there's nothing really significant, but here it is."

"How about Andrew Weiss?" I asked. "Is there anything specific about him?"

"Well, Andrew Weiss is sort of a mystery man," said Tim. "Nobody seems to know much about him."

"Yeah, I've gotten that impression. And he's probably not important to the case anyway, but he makes me curious. Here's a guy with some pretty strong beliefs and opinions, none of which I agree with, for what that's worth, but personally he's a complete zero. Why all the secrecy? If he believes this shit, why not stand up and be counted?"

Tim shrugged. "Maybe the cause is the important thing to him," he said. "Maybe he thinks he can accomplish more with anonymity than by a cult of personality."

"Wrong. He's already a personality cult, only it's based on a faceless person. Andrew Weiss probably isn't even his real name. Andrew. That means 'man,' doesn't it?"

Tim nodded. "From the Greek *anthropos*, I think."

"And Weiss is German for white, isn't it? Andrew Weiss. Man white. White man. Pretty theatrical."

"Or maybe it's just his name." He smiled. "Maybe you're investing way too much meaning into all this."

"Maybe. But I appreciate you downloading this stuff for me." I put my hand on the pile of pinfeed paper and sighed. "I'm going to spend tonight going over it and hope it tells me something that will help."

"I hope it does." Tim's eyes grew serious again. "You let me know if there's any other way I can help. If someone did kill Cass, I want to see them found and punished. And if all you find out is that it was a terrible and regrettable accident, at least Peter and Nora will have some peace of mind."

"Yes, and I can't say I'd be sorry if you turned out to be right. I don't like to think about the implications of a bunch of anonymous hooded murderers leading double lives as ordinary citizens of Cedar Ridge."

Our lunch came, and it was everything Desmond Gunn had promised. Tim allowed Desmond to pour him a glass of wine, but I noticed that he didn't drink any after the first, customary taste. I drank two glasses and wished I could take the rest home. The Rosemount Shiraz was an adventuresome vintage. Desmond chose us a dessert, heavy on chocolate, and had a waiter serve us cups of strong coffee.

"So how's it going so far?" Tim asked. "Have you come up with anything interesting?"

I filled him in on what I'd learned since yesterday, including the revelations on the videotape of the second A.R.C. demonstration. "Cass ID'd that guy, even with the hood and robe on. It had to be someone she knew well or had some sort of regular dealings with. If he knew she'd made him, and if he was scared, he could be the key to this whole thing. I'm burning up to know who he is."

"You couldn't recognize him?"

"Well, I haven't met everyone in town yet, and the hood's a

pretty good disguise, all things considered. Now the one who was doing all the talking, I think if I studied his voice, I might be able to match it up with a face eventually." I planned to watch the video a few more times and listen carefully to that voice. "The other guy—the one Cass knew—I don't know about him. He hardly said anything."

"Sounds to me like he said too much," said Tim.

When we finished our coffee and dessert, Tim drove me back to the *Sentinel* and I took my rental car for a drive. As I drove east from town on Black Mountain Road, I passed the Emergency Medical Center, reset the trip odometer, and glanced at my watch. Several minutes later I spotted the new guardrail that marked the spot where Cass Lowry had left the road late on the previous Friday night, near a county road marker.

I checked my watch and the odometer again before I found a wide spot to park the car. After waiting for a couple of vehicles to go by, I walked across the highway to the fatal spot and stood there looking down.

The distance between life and death, as the crow flies, is a short one. One second you're walking across the street, and the next you're lying under a crosstown bus. For Cass Lowry the distance had been perhaps fifty feet, the depth of the boulder-lined gorge on the other side of the guardrail. There was no debris, of course, and no sign that anything had happened except for some scrub oak and other shrubbery that had been broken off by the impact. Still, I imagined I could see the wreckage on the rocks below, dust rising in eerie silence.

A truck sped by behind me, raising a wind that pushed me against the flimsy strip of sheet metal. I gasped and grabbed the railing with my hands as my knees gave out momentarily, then pulled myself up and dusted myself off.

As I turned around I saw that a car had parked behind mine. The driver looked at me for a moment, then checked the road behind him and pulled away. I recognized him as the same man who had nodded to me in the bookstore parking lot. His razor-sharp features were unmistakable.

CHAPTER 16

IN A SMALL TOWN YOU SEE THE SAME FEW PEOPLE OVER AND over again. Until you get used to it, it seems strange, like being followed. In this case, however, I figured I really was being followed, and not only by Judy Roy. I determined to keep an eye out for this guy from now on.

I drove back into town and straight to the Big Grizzly Towing Company. Kingdom Neary was in his office filling out a trip log. He smiled broadly when he looked up and saw me. "What can I do for you, ma'am?" he inquired, motioning me to the guest chair and abusing the soda machine to get me a drink.

"You told me the other day that the ambulance arrived at the scene of Cass Lowry's accident in two minutes flat," I said, popping the tab on my drink. "Was that an exaggeration?"

"Not by much. I figured they must have busted speed records coming up that hill. Takes about ten minutes to get up there from the Emergency Center, and that's traveling at a pretty good clip."

"I made it in twelve and eleven today. And it would take them a couple of minutes to be ready to respond, I'd imagine."

"Yep, and I know it wasn't much more than five minutes after I called that I saw them. They came right after the deputies." He looked up and behind me. "Hey, Mike."

"Hey, King," Mike McCutcheon replied. He sauntered over to the desk and sat down on the corner, swinging one leg and smiling at me. "You do get around, Miss Caley Burke." The smile took on a hint of insolence. "I've been hoping I'd see you up at the Overlook one of these evenings. It's the happening place in this town. I'd be happy to buy you a drink or two anytime you stop by."

"I've been busy." I forced a smile. "So, did your car get towed?"

"Oh, me and Kingdom have a sort of back-scratching business arrangement. When an old car gets put out to pasture around here, he's usually the first to know it."

"And you're on the spot to reap the parts."

"I am indeed." He looked pleased that I had remembered his hobby, as though it might be a sign that I was interested in something else about him. "Take a look at what I drove here in," he said, pointing out the window. A shiny red and white sedan with matching leather upholstery gleamed in the sunlight just outside the office window. "Fifty-four Chevy Bel-Air," Mike informed me, bursting with pride.

I had to admit the car was a beauty. Compact and sporty, it was a success on its own terms. Restored to showroom newness, it seemed still to exist in a time when the longer, sleeker models with tail fins and too much chrome were mere pencil drawings cluttering a designer's desk. "It's very nice," I told him, nodding approval.

"How about a spin around town?" He'd moved closer while I wasn't paying attention, and his arm brushed up against mine. I didn't find the contact particularly pleasant.

I moved away. "Sorry. I'm really pretty busy." Mike moved in again, grinning like a friendly predator.

"Was that all you needed to know, Ms. Burke?" Kingdom asked me.

"That's it," I said. "You were very helpful, thanks."

"Any time at all," he said, moving between me and Mike. He took my arm and escorted me outside. "I swear that guy never gives up," he said when we were out of earshot. "He scores a lot at the bars, but he never seems to notice when a woman isn't interested. You have a real nice day, Ms. Burke."

"Thanks. And thanks for helping out." I got into the car.

Kingdom closed the door and put his huge hands on the window frame. "Oh, you would have handled him yourself, but I suspect in your line of work you have to worry about being rude to folks you might need to get something out of later. I was just keeping the wheels greased for you."

"You're a gem, Kingdom," I told him.

"A diamond in the rough, my mama used to say," he acknowledged.

I pulled out and found a spot between two motor homes heading toward the center of town. When I had gone about a mile, I turned off into a paved parking area near a complex of office buildings and shut off the car's engine. The heat beat on the windows, impatient to have its way with me. I got out and let it slam into me. I sighed. I was getting spoiled by air conditioning.

Maureen Adler's real estate office stood out like a sore thumb (in a lovely shade of sore-thumb pink) amid a row of gray and butternut-tan buildings shaded by huge old oak trees. When I walked in, Maureen was clearing papers from her desk into pristine pink file folders and placing them into file drawers.

"Are you closing up now?" I asked.

She looked up at me, and there was a half-second of blankness in her eyes before her brain found my folder. "Ms. Burke! So you've developed an interest in Cedar Ridge real estate after all!"

"A piece here and there," I admitted. I looked out Maureen's window and up the highway about two blocks to the corner where the A.R.C. had demonstrated twice this year. "Who owns that corner there?" I asked, pointing.

"A conglomerate in Sacramento. And there's no use trying to get your hands on it—they're buying up that entire block to put up one of those big chain hotels. It's going to be just wonderful, you wait and see."

"Who rents the corner, then? The lot with the souvenir shop on it?"

"Oh, that's Bert and Alice Trout. They've lived here and owned that business for just years and years. They sold the land to the Sacramento investors a few months ago, and they're building a new store on a site I sold them and renting the old one month-to-month until it's finished."

"Isn't that the corner where the A.R.C. demonstrated?"

"Oh, you've heard about that? Yes, I think Bert and Alice gave them permission to park their cars behind the store and use the corner. They were perfectly lawful demonstrations, you know."

"I know. But it's hard for many people to support their views."

"Well, Cass and her bunch certainly didn't," Maureen said with a little shake of her shoulders. "They tried to turn this town into some kind of circus over a couple of little political gatherings. What with those petitions of theirs on the counters in more than a dozen businesses hereabouts, they were scaring off potential home buyers in droves.

"And the Sacramento people who want to put up the hotel? They were scared to death. I had my work cut out for me talking them out of dumping the whole deal. They're still a little nervous about all the publicity. Cass Lowry nearly cost this town the most important thing that's happened to it in twenty years."

And the most important thing that had happened to Maureen Adler, too, I'd be willing to bet. Tim had said Maureen was headed for the real estate big time, but it was evident that only in a pond this small could she ever be anything more than a very small frog. She stayed in Cedar Ridge because she could shine here, to mix a couple of metaphors. This hotel deal was her chance to shine, and no doubt to make a bundle of money, and Cass had nearly cocked it up for her.

"Don't you think the presence of the A.R.C. would have scared them, all by itself?" I asked. "I mean the sight of a couple of dozen guys in hoods might spook anybody."

"Honey, those people wouldn't even have been on that corner passing out pamphlets if it weren't for the way this town has changed in the past few years. You can't appreciate this, coming from outside, but this used to be such a nice town."

"It's not a nice town anymore?"

"Well, I guess not. There are coloreds here and Jews and . . . well, a lot of people who don't share our values." Her voice lowered to a whisper. "Homosexuals, and people like that." She filed the last of the pink folders and took a handbag off the back of her chair. "It never used to be that way when I was growing up here. Those kinds of people stayed away from places like this, and that's the way we liked it."

"It must be hell on real estate values," I commented drily.

Maureen sighed as she rose and patted the wrinkles from her pink linen skirt. "Honey, you can't imagine. We want our town to grow and be prosperous, and opportunities like that hotel deal are the kind of thing that will make that happen, not an influx of minorities and perverts."

I managed a smile to hide my true sentiments from Maureen, not that I figured she was all that skillful at social signals. "Well, I won't keep you from getting out of here," I said. "I'll take one of these pamphlets about the houses for sale, and I'll get out of your hair."

"No trouble at all. You let me know if there's anything you want to take a look at—I'll drive you there personally."

"You bet," I said, waving goodbye with the pamphlet.

The air seemed a little fresher outside Maureen Adler's office. I got into my car just as Maureen came out and locked up. She gave me a little wave as she climbed into her (predictably) pink Cadillac. I sat in the lot and watched her drive off.

It was easy to see that Maureen had a lot of sympathy for Andrew Weiss's supporters—after all, she had a vested interest in keeping real estate values high in Cedar Ridge, and a personal interest in making sure her world stayed small and her mind narrow. Here we were, dancing on the brink of the twenty-first century, but some things never seemed to change. I was suddenly very tired, but there was still one more visit I wanted to make.

Mountain Arts Collectibles and Treasures was a sickly yellow building set back by the length of a generous parking lot from the corner of Highway 49 and Cedar Avenue. I parked my car next to a minivan piled high with camping equipment and stood in the afternoon heat, looking around the lot and nearby streets for hatchet-faced men in blue sedans. The coast was clear.

As I looked around, a strange feeling of familiarity washed over me. This was the place I had seen in the videotape, teeming with A.R.C. demonstrators in embroidered white robes. I was standing only a few feet from the spot where Cass Lowry had confronted the hooded men. For a moment it was like they were all around, watching me through their dark eye-holes. An involuntary shudder passed through me.

I ducked into the store and shivered at the nip of refrigerated air. A few small windows let in a minimum of natural light, which was augmented by fluorescent ceiling fixtures that buzzed just along the top range of my hearing like mosquitoes from Hell and bathed the store in a cold gray light. Several gondola fixtures of sparkling glass shelves held the more respectable merchandise, and the walls were crowded with gaudy plaster and plastic junk items and fringed tapestries featuring Elvis and poker-playing dogs. A handful of tourists walked up and down aisles picking up and appraising the merchandise.

"Looking for something special?" A middle-aged woman in a denim skirt and blouse bedecked with ersatz Southwest Indian jewelry smiled a welcoming smile.

"Just wanted to pick up some souvenirs for the folks at home," I said.

"Well, you look around all you want," she said, waving a hand at the merchandise. "And if you need anything, just yell for Alice."

"I'll do that," I promised, and started down an aisle of hand-painted ceramic coffee mugs and ashtrays adorned with "Cedar Ridge" and "California Gold Country" in glaring gold ink. Further down the row, mountain quails, poppies, and grizzly bears continued the "I Visited California" theme.

I was pondering a set of salt and pepper shakers in the shape of cedar trees when I heard a voice call out from the back room: "Alice, where the hell is that invoice from Tuesday's glassware shipment?" It was a man's voice—high, piping, and querulous. Little. High-pitched. That's how Gordon Terrell had described the voice of one of his attackers.

I walked as casually as possible toward the source of the voice. A tiny man, skinny as a stick-figure, with wispy gray hair and mousy features, strode from the office doorway in front of me, clutching a fistful of packing slips. I jumped back. He executed a 90-degree turn and headed down another aisle, oblivious to my presence. "Alice!" he shrilled. "I can't find that goddamned invoice!"

"Not in front of the customers, Bert!"

I peeked through a bar-glass display and watched them while pretending to choose between highball glasses adorned with hunkering gold miners and hand-blown cedar tree swizzle sticks. Alice towered over Bert by a good six inches, even in her flat shoes. She patted his arm and spoke to him in calming tones as one might pacify a spooked horse, or in Bert's case perhaps Shetland pony would have been a more apt simile. In a few moments, after pointing out the missing invoice in his hand, she had him ready for the halter.

"Now, why couldn't I find that goddamned thing?" Bert said, scratching his balding head. "I'm no good at this office stuff, Alice—I've told you that for years."

"Well, you're no good at the customer stuff either, Bert," Alice reminded him gently, "so why don't you go back and wrestle with those invoices some more?" She turned him around and gave him a gentle shove in the direction of the back room.

I had to get Gordon Terrell in here to hear that voice, I decided. And I'd talk to Danny, too—it could have been the same crowd that jumped him a while back. I picked up a couple of cedar tree coffee mugs for Jake and Terrie and started for the cash register.

A young man walked into the store. He sauntered up to me and paused, looking me up and down with a half-leer. He was wearing a white T-shirt with a pack of Marlboros rolled into the sleeve, apparently unaware of what a cliché he was making of himself, and an outdated one at that. Under the edge of the cigarette pack I saw a tattoo: the word MAN in bold block letters below the shoulder. I resisted the urge to pull up the sleeve and see the modifier.

I turned away and pretended to be interested in a display of postcards. He walked up to the register.

"Hi there, Dale," said Alice.

"Hi, Alice. Bert around?"

"He sure is, honey. He's in the back there." The man walked into the office without knocking and closed the door. Dale. Dale Reid? He was about the right age, I thought. Unusual that he would hang with a guy like Bert Trout, unless of course they had some common interests, such as dressing up in hoods and beating up people whose looks they didn't like.

I tore my gaze away from the office door before I could be seen as staring, and put my purchases on the counter by the register. Alice Trout made small talk while she wrapped the mugs in tissue paper and placed them in gift boxes. I kept sneaking peeks at the office, wondering what was going on back there and if it had anything to do with my case. There was no remotely graceful way to find out, so I paid for my souvenirs and walked outside.

This time the blue car was there, parked at the far end of the lot. The slender, dark man with the severe features watched me get into my car. I decided there was no reason to panic yet. He could be watching me for the A.R.C., but as long as all he did was watch, there was exactly nothing I could do about it.

As I checked my car mirrors, a shiny white pickup caught my eye. I pulled my car around and looked at it. It looked a lot like the same truck that had been playing dodge 'em with me on the road from Sacramento—an older model with a shitty white paint job. There were also a few badly hammered dents in one fender. Just looking at it made my heart jump once, remembering the close call. What a wacko. I wondered if the guy was a local or some tourist passing through on his way to an accident.

I pulled out onto the highway and the dark man pulled out two cars behind me. I drove to Cass's house, checking the mirror now and again for the blue sedan. He stayed with me all the way to the dirt road. One thing for sure, I wasn't going to get lonely in Cedar Ridge; the local Welcome Wagon was working overtime.

CHAPTER 17

NO ONE WAS AROUND WHEN I LET MYSELF INTO THE HOUSE. Peter's car was in the driveway, so he was probably in his studio, a converted garage next to the house, with skylights and windows all over the north and east sides. I thought it was probably good for him to get to work again as soon as possible, and I didn't want to disturb him now.

Nora wouldn't close the bookstore for another hour at least, so I was alone with my thoughts. After a very few minutes of that, I picked up the phone and called David.

"You've reached the home of Antonio Garza and David Hayden," David's voice said. I started to hang up, but I wasn't ready to stop listening to his voice yet. "Neither Tony nor David can come to the phone right now, so when you hear the beep, please leave a message and we'll return your call as soon as possible." I sighed. I'd forgotten that David said he'd be gone until tomorrow. The machine beeped, but I was too depressed to say anything.

I looked up Danny Abrahams's phone number and called him. "Tell me about the guys who tried to beat you up," I said. "There were five of them?"

"That's my best guess."

"Do you remember anything about their voices?"

"Let's see. Mean. Nasty. Not nice. Oh, yeah, one had a little squeaky voice."

"Do you know anyone in town who has a voice like that?"

He was silent for a moment. "No," he said. "Of course my social circle is limited."

"How about people you might deal with in town?"

"No, I think I'd remember that voice. That's the only time I ever heard it."

"What did he look like?"

"Like a guy with a hood."

"Not his face, wiseguy, just in general."

"He was the shortest one of them, I'm pretty sure of that. He wasn't very tall."

Bingo. "You free tomorrow? I'd like to take you someplace to meet someone. You might find it interesting."

"I'll be here all day—just me and my keyboard. My car's in the shop, though."

"I'll come by and get you. I'll call first."

I went upstairs to the guest room and sat in the easy chair with Tim's printouts and a glass of cold lemonade. Most of it was familiar by now, more familiar than I had ever wanted such things to be.

Andrew Weiss had sprung from the void with the publication of his first book, *Let's Bring Back America*, sold mostly through mail-order ads in outer fringe publications. The book contained a call to arms, literally, aimed at lower- to middle-class northern European whites, to organize chapters of the American Rescue Coalition and raise money for the kinds of causes Andrew Weiss supported. Guns were an important part of the Weiss philosophy, since the downtrodden white race was expecting a shooting war with blacks, Hispanics, and who knew all, just any day now.

Weiss himself was a complete blank, the articles pointed out: no known photographs, not even a physical address—just a post-office box that had been traced to a Los Angeles mailing service that maintained a number of such boxes around the Los Angeles area. Since the mail was forwarded and the service guaranteed confidentiality, it was another dead end in the search for Weiss's true identity.

By the time I waded through the printouts, the light was

failing and there were welcome people-noises coming from downstairs. I went to join them.

Matt and Harry streaked by me on their way to the back yard, almost bowling me over. "Boys!" their mother shouted at them, but they were long gone before the sound could reach them. The back screen door creaked shut behind the sound of their laughter.

"I'm glad they've stopped being so quiet," I said to Nora. "They're five-year-old boys again."

"I'm glad you understand," Nora said, smiling. "I know you're probably not used to having children around." She hefted two bags of groceries from the entry hall floor and carried them to the kitchen. I grabbed two more and followed her.

"I don't have any of my own, but I confess to a fondness for the species. Teenagers, too. Strange, huh?"

"Was that a deliberate decision, not having children, or just the way things have worked out so far? I remember when you were married to Michael you tried to have a family." My ex-husband, Michael Carlson, still lived about six blocks away from me in Cascade, and we were friendly acquaintances if not actually friends. Our marriage had been a disastrous mistake for both of us, and neither had ventured into matrimony since our divorce a little more than three years previous.

"The way things have worked out, period," I said. "I'm thirty-two and change. My attempts at having children in my twenties nearly wrecked my mental health. I'm not going to start planning a family at this point." I didn't mention it to Nora, but I had nourished quite a few thoughts along those lines recently, and life had slapped me hard for my trouble. It would be a while before I allowed myself those dreams again, if ever.

"How's your day been, so far?" Nora asked as she placed food in the refrigerator. "Besides hot, I mean."

"Oh, let's see—productive, dangerous, curious, and downright interesting." I reached up and touched my forehead, aware of a headache that had been lurking for hours just beyond my perception; my punishment for enjoying the wine this afternoon, no doubt. I picked up a bottle of pain relievers from the countertop where Nora had set them, and swallowed three, washing them down with a glass of water from the tap.

"I've got some printouts on the A.R.C. up in the guest room that we could go over. And then there's the rundown of my day. Would you like to hear that now?"

Nora shook her head. She pulled a bottle of Syrah from a grocery bag and took two glasses from an overhead rack. "Let's go in the living room and kick back first. We'll wait until Peter gets in from the studio for the serious stuff."

I was looking forward to the wine and grateful for Nora's consideration. There's always plenty of time for the serious stuff.

I stared up into the darkness and tried to find a comfortable position; I'd tried them all in the past hour and a half, but sleep wouldn't come to me. There was a lot going on in this town, a strong undercurrent flowing beneath the peaceful, friendly exterior.

My reading about the American Rescue Coalition earlier that day hadn't done a lot to relax me. Apparently based somewhere in Los Angeles, the A.R.C. had been growing steadily since the publication of Andrew Weiss's first book; the one I'd just finished reading.

Since most copies of *Let's Bring Back America*, his second book, *The White Man's Way*, and two dozen political pamphlets were sold through mail order, there were no accurate sales figures. It was estimated, however, that there were over a million copies of each book in circulation, and double or triple that on the pamphlets. "Let's Bring Back America" bumper stickers were sprouting up like fungus, especially in depressed rural areas, but there were plenty of them to be found wherever you cared to look.

Small chapters of the A.R.C. were becoming larger and getting more public with every passing month. Chapter leaders, one article maintained, received a monthly newsletter from Andrew Weiss, informing them of strategy and tactics for "spreading the word and the way" in their own hometowns, and naming politicians to be supported or denounced. Violence associated with A.R.C. activities was increasing, including violence against the A.R.C. demonstrators themselves.

Peter and Nora had listened grimly to my synopsis of the articles. They knew most of this stuff already; it was me who needed educating. Now I knew more than I ever wanted to know about the mindset of white supremacists and the horrible ease with which people latched on to their ideas.

I had told Peter and Nora about my trip to Sacramento and my visit to Bert and Alice Trout's store. I'd left out my conversation with Maureen Adler; I didn't feel like going into her narrow-minded whining and sniping at Cass for opposing the American Rescue Coalition.

I did include Danny's description of the squeaky-voiced man. So far, this was our biggest lead to the A.R.C., and an unknown someone involved with the A.R.C. was in turn our prime suspect in Cass's murder. We had experienced a moment of elation at the thought of a lead; then we all seemed to remember at once the purpose of the investigation, and that took all the joy out of it.

I made a few half-hearted attempts to adjust pillows, then sat up and put on the robe I had left at the foot of the bed. I switched on the bedside lamp. Across the room I could see the videocassette on the dresser where I had left it. I picked it up on my way out and went downstairs.

It was dark in the living room except for a small light that was always kept on in the kitchen. I put the tape into the VCR and turned the volume down so I wouldn't wake anyone upstairs. I had mentioned my talk with Rocky Marx to Peter and Nora earlier in the evening, but I didn't think they were ready to see this tape just yet, so I didn't suggest playing it. Now I picked up the remote control and fast-forwarded to Cass's encounter with the A.R.C.

I sat in the seat nearest the television and listened to the voice of the first hooded man without being able to match it with any I had heard in the last few days. I watched Cass react to the second man without recognizing anything familiar in him myself. I ran the tape back and watched the same footage over again. Just into the third viewing, I was aware of another person in the room. I turned to look.

Peter stood in the kitchen doorway, silhouetted in the soft glow. Flickers of light from the television screen touched his face and reflected on the tears that rolled down his cheeks.

I hit the stop button. "Peter, I'm so sorry. I thought you were asleep."

He let out a ragged breath. "It's okay. I came down to get myself a drink. Would you like one?"

"Okay." How could I have been so stupid? I knew Peter wasn't sleeping very well. How could I be so careless as to put him through this? I felt like a total ass.

Peter got ice and glasses from the kitchen and poured me a shot of white rum, then took a bottle of Scotch from the cabinet and sank down wearily in a leather chair. "Tomorrow night it'll be a week," he said. "Do you know, sometimes I still don't believe it really happened? I wander down here at night half-expecting to find Cass watching an old movie on TV. That's what she used to do when she couldn't sleep. So I saw the TV on, and someone was sitting there . . . and then I saw it was you and what you were watching . . ." He poured whisky into his glass and lifted the glass to his lips with hands that trembled slightly.

I felt like shit, but there was nothing I could say that would make either of us feel any better, and finally the moment for saying anything at all was past. We sat and drank in silence. A dog howled outside in the distance, then another dog, closer by, picked up the song. Were they communicating in some way, or just feeling lonely together?

"No matter how close you think you are to someone, there are always things that get left unsaid," Peter said finally. He sat in shadow on the opposite sofa, speaking softly into the gloom of the darkened living room.

"Maybe that's because we assume there'll always be time to say them," I offered.

"We have to assume that," Peter said, sitting forward into the faint light from the kitchen. "If you think too much about the inevitability of death, you'll go nuts."

"Or at least miss the chance to enjoy life," I noted. Old Mister Death had certainly been in my thoughts a lot lately, like a grief temporarily forgotten that comes rushing back to remind you that all is not well in your world. The unalterable forgone conclusion to all life hovered just over my left shoulder lately, tapping me with a bony finger when I threatened to forget his presence.

"I wanted to get married," Peter said, taking another healthy swallow of his Scotch. "Cass had gotten such a bad deal the first time around, she wasn't sure whether marriage itself might be the thing that turned people against one another."

I sighed. "I've wondered the same thing myself a time or two."

"There was time to work it out, you know? There was plenty of time to decide what we wanted to do. Only there wasn't." He set the glass down and refilled it from the bottle. "Well, why the hell not? *I* didn't go anywhere!" Tears invaded his voice and he sat back, silent again for a minute or more.

The dead are forever beyond our reach. We can't say the unsaid things to them, and nothing's going to get worked out. I wished I could say something different to Peter, but it would be bullshit and he'd know it.

"I'm just so goddamned angry," he said finally. "I can't forgive her for dying and cheating me out of the rest of our life together."

I leaned across the carpet and touched his arm. "When you do," I said, "this will all get a lot easier."

When I finished my drink and went upstairs, Peter was still sitting in the near-dark, staring at the blank TV screen.

CHAPTER 18

I SLEPT BADLY AND WOKE EARLIER THAN I WANTED TO. I lay in bed with my eyes closed, and bits and pieces of things recombined almost randomly in my mind. A white pickup with a bad paint job; Dale Reid (Nora had confirmed my identification) walking into Bert Trout's office like he owned the place; Maureen Adler's whining "there goes the neighborhood"; Kingdom Neary looking down a fifty-foot drop at what was left of a little white car. A white pickup with a bad paint job.

I sat up in bed. "Jesus, I must have been totally unconscious to miss that!" I said aloud. I pulled on jeans and a fresh shirt and slipped into sandals. Grimacing into the mirror, I brushed my teeth and combed my hair, then grabbed my handbag and ran out of the room. I almost knocked Peter down as I turned the corner and started down the stairs.

"What's up?" he asked.

"Is there coffee in the kitchen? I need to think."

"Nora forgot to buy some. Can I buy you a cup in town?"

"Sure. I think I might be on to something, Peter. Maybe something big."

"Let's go, then. I'll leave a note for Nora."

It was barely seven when we got to the Coffee Pot, but all the tables in the smoking section were filled with locals grabbing a cup on their way to work and a few truck drivers whose rigs idled outside while they got some breakfast into them. The non-smoking section was practically empty, and Peter and I seated ourselves at a table in the back, ignoring the "Please Wait to be Seated" sign.

Tom Flanders brought over a vacuum pot of coffee and two cups. "You folks look like you could use this," he said with a smile. "I'll come back and take your order in just a minute."

I poured the coffee and drank the first cup in three gulps. Peter stared in the direction of his cup, eyes unfocused in thought. "What's up?" I asked.

"I think I got a little out of hand last night," he said. "I'm sorry I unloaded on you that way."

I put my hand on his. "Peter, I've been unloaded on by experts. The only thing that happened last night was that you admitted something that was eating you up. You had to do it eventually, you know."

"I know. But it doesn't make me any less embarrassed about my behavior."

"It'll be easier if you think of me as a friend."

A smile creased his face. "Right now you're the best friend this family's got."

"I'm the only investigator in your address book. You'd get the same service from a stranger."

"But a stranger wouldn't care. You do."

I nodded. I cared a lot about the case and the people and the principles involved. Murder was a nasty act regardless of who the victim was, and the murder of a good person who'd never deliberately harmed anyone was inconceivable at the emotional level. It meant a lot more to me than just another case to find out who had killed Cass Lowry, and why. Now I had a couple of new connections to work with, and I was eager to get started.

"Maybe you can help me think," I said to Peter as I refilled my cup. "My brain is wrecked from lack of sleep, but things are starting to come together." I reached into my handbag and pulled out my notebook. One by one I pulled all the little pages free from their spiral binding. Tiny bits of paper rained down over the table as I ripped out pages and arranged them in front of me.

"Cass pissed off some people in town," I said, pushing a piece of paper forward. "We don't know who for sure, but we know they threatened her life."

I fingered another piece of paper. "She recognized some-body at the second A.R.C. picnic over there on the corner. He knew she'd ID'd him. Six days later the accident happened." I held up my hand as Peter started to protest. "I don't think it was an accident either, but that's the official call."

"The tow truck driver called the ambulance," I said, rearranging a third slip. "They got there faster than humanly possible. That means someone called them before Kingdom Neary did. And the sheriff's deputies arrived even before the ambulance, which means someone called them too."

"Is that significant?"

"Not if it was someone who saw the car leave the road by chance and drove to the nearest phone and reported it. But if someone forced Cass off the road, it was most likely that person who made the call."

"Why do that if they were trying to kill her anyway?"

I stared into space for a moment, rearranging my thoughts. "Maybe they weren't. Maybe they wanted to spook her, and things got out of control. Maybe whatever Cass did to upset someone wasn't actually enough to make them murder her, but enough to make them warn her."

"The Andrew Weiss crowd had already warned her she'd be dead if she didn't back off."

"I know. Who else may have warned her about something? Maybe not so overtly."

"I don't know what you mean."

"How were Cass's relations with Maureen Adler?"

"Mostly friendly on the outside."

"And on the inside?"

"Maybe a little less friendly. Maureen is such an obvious phony it's easy to tell when she doesn't like someone, even when she's gushing all over them. That's how she was with Cass, and Cass wasn't fooled by it."

"Did Cass ever come into actual conflict with Maureen?"

Peter looked thoughtful. "I do remember Cass told me one time that Maureen had come into the store and ranted about Cass and the gang scaring off someone—investors, maybe. It didn't seem important at the time, so I don't really remember the details. Cass thought it was a real hoot." He smiled, remembering.

"Maureen has been setting up a multimillion dollar real estate deal for the corner at Highway 49 and Cedar Avenue," I said. "She has some cash cows in Sacramento interested in buying up the whole block for a hotel, and she's looking to collect a chunk of money in commissions."

"I remember hearing about the hotel deal, but talk has backed off a lot the last couple of months."

"So did Maureen's investors. It was all the publicity over Cass and the A.R.C. Maureen was solidly pissed about it when I talked to her yesterday."

"At Cass?"

"Yes. For arranging the Sacramento TV coverage, writing letters to the papers, and bringing the whole thing to public attention."

"I don't understand," said Peter. "Why not get pissed at the A.R.C.?"

"Simple. She *likes* those guys. She thinks they're good for what's bad for Cedar Ridge, and what's bad for Cedar Ridge, particularly as it affects the value of real estate, is bad for Maureen Adler."

"You don't think . . ."

"I don't know what to think. It bears looking into, though, doesn't it?" My head was spinning. First the Weiss crowd with their threats and intimidation; now Maureen Adler at risk of losing a small fortune. So many people with so much stake in maintaining the status quo, and someone with enough stake to commit murder.

I sighed. "And that isn't even what woke me up this morning," I said. "There's more." I searched the table for another slip of paper. "Yesterday, on my way back up the hill, a truck pulled a couple of weird stunts in a passing lane. Later I saw what I think was the same truck parked outside Bert and Alice Trout's tourist trap.

"Damn! I wish I'd taken a look at that guy on the highway. All I could think of was getting the hell away from there. I thought he was just a shitty driver." I looked up at Peter. "It was a pickup with a brand-new paint job. When I looked at it at Mountain Arts—providing it was the same truck—it had dents in the right front fender. Does that match any car in town you're familiar with?"

"Pickups are as common as rocks around here," Peter said.

"Most of the people in the store looked like tourists," I said, remembering. "And I don't think the truck was there when I pulled up, but I can't be sure. Dale Reid came in just before I left, and then I saw the white truck."

"I don't know what kind of car he drives. Maybe Nora does."

"Mark Birdsall knows what Reid was driving a couple of months ago," I reminded Peter, "and he might remember what shape the paint job was in at the time, too. If someone really ran Cass off the road, they may have damaged their car doing it. The dents in this guy's fender had been hammered out a bit, but not professionally, and there was a new coat of paint that looked like it was slapped on in a hurry."

"Cass's car was totally demolished," Peter said. "Even if there were marks from another car, they could be lost in all the other damage."

"Especially if no one was really looking for evidence."

"Or if the other car was white. Maureen drives that hideous pink Cadillac, but she could have another car at home. And you saw a white truck with a new paint job."

"A real hurry-up kind of paint job," I said. "A lot of dust, and badly applied. Where in this town is there a place where you could have someone paint your car in a hurry?"

"Not that I know of," said Peter.

"I imagine most people get their cars painted at one of the big chain operations in Sacramento," I said. "But this wasn't that careful a job." I gathered up my little slips of paper and stuffed them back into the notebook. "We should check out Maureen's house and grounds, and talk to Mark Birdsall about Dale Reid's truck. We also have to round up

Gordon and Danny and see if they can ID Bert Trout."

I looked up to see Tom Flanders standing over us with an order pad in his hand. "You guys ready for some breakfast?"

Peter looked at his watch. "We might as well, Tom. We're up too early for anything else."

CHAPTER 19

. . . .

"I WISH THERE WERE SOME WAY TO FOLLOW UP ON EVERY-thing at once," I told Peter as we lingered over coffee, waiting for anyone besides the birds and the truckers to be up and about.

"I don't know about all at once, but we can cut the time in half," he said. "Drop me off back at the house and I'll take my car out and we'll split up the work. I can check out Maureen's and talk to Mark. You get Danny and Gordon and take them by Bert Trout's store. I have some drawings to send off this afternoon, so I'll have to be home in time to finish them and pack them up before the FedEx man comes."

"Well, that should be a morning's work. Thanks, Peter. If the Bert Trout connection is solid, I'll have to start watching him. It'd be good to have a tail on Dale, too, if he didn't already know about me. Sooner or later, one of them is going to do something revealing or lead us to someone else. We don't have to nail the perp ourselves, but we need one good, solid piece of evidence to reopen the case."

"Maybe we'll find that piece today," said Peter. The look in his eyes was part hope, part fury.

A quick call to Danny found him at home as promised, and another to Gordon Terrell got me the promise of an hour between nine and ten to pay a visit to the Trouts. Leaving the Coffee Pot, I picked up the dark man again in my side mirror. I resisted the urge to give him a cheery wave as he pulled out of the parking lot and settled in three cars behind me. These A.R.C. bozos were tiresome, but consistent.

Peter had drawn me a map to Danny's place northeast of town. A narrow, twisted ribbon of blacktop took off from Black Mountain Road and led up and down over several hills to an even narrower dirt road and a ranch gate that Danny had told me would be unlocked. It was, and I drove through, leaving it open for the return trip. The dark man drove on by.

Ahead, a Pennsylvania Dutch farmhouse commanded a gentle rise covered with native grasses and wildflowers. A more deliberate garden surrounded the two visible sides of the house, making a riot of shape and color against the white of the house walls. Danny sat outside on an old wooden glider, freshly painted in emerald-green enamel. A laptop computer sat on his knees and a grizzled basset hound was stretched out nearby. When I opened the car door, the dog staggered to his feet and bayed hoarsely at the intrusion.

"Save your energy, Oppie," said Danny. "You never know when you might have to chase a rabbit or something."

"You have quite a security force there," I said, coming up onto the porch and holding out my hand for the basset to sniff.

"This is Dr. Robert Oppenheimer," said Danny by way of introduction, "and his loyalty is more theoretical than substantial. He once *licked* a burglar to death, though." He shook his head sadly. "It wasn't pretty."

"I'll bet not." I took a seat on one end of the glider and pointed to the computer. "Bread and butter work?" I asked. "Or is it your book?"

Danny nodded. "Peter told you about the book."

"I hope that's all right. I know it's kind of personal, but I guess he thought I'd understand."

"Of course it's all right," said Danny. "And to answer your question, I'm working on an article for a gardening magazine. 'Low-Maintenance Perennials for Shady Places.'" He smiled ruefully and closed the computer with a soft snap. "The book I take up and abandon by turns. I'm still too close to the subject matter."

"Is that why you left San Francisco? Because of your friend?"

"Because of a lot of friends," said Danny. He got up and put the computer inside the house, then closed and locked the door. "They call it 'The City That Waits to Die,'" he said, turning and walking down the steps with me.

"The problem seems to be too many people aren't waiting anymore."

Gordon met us in the parking lot of Mountain Arts at nine on the dot.

"Danny boy," Gordon greeted him with a wide grin. "How's that lazy old dog?" Gordon knew everyone by their animal population, it seemed.

"Old and lazy, mainly," Danny replied. "You ever been in this place before?" He indicated the hideous yellow building with distaste.

Gordon's look echoed Danny's repugnance. "This must be the ugliest place in town, next to Maureen Adler's real estate office," he said. "I'd remember if I'd been here before."

"You'd probably still be having nightmares about it," Danny agreed.

"Well, let's check out the souvenirs of Cedar Ridge," I suggested. "We may find something in here we simply must have."

"Speak for yourself," said Gordon as he stepped through the door into the exhibit of wall-to-wall kitsch. I walked ahead of him and Danny and casually led the way, past the few shoppers that were already scoping out keepsakes, back to the vicinity of the office. The door was closed.

"What do you want?" said a woman's voice behind us. I turned to face Alice Trout, arrayed today in a bright turquoise dress and a different batch of faux jewelry. She scowled down at me, arms crossed in front of her chest, feet planted wide and ready for action. This was not a happy woman I was looking up at, and not at all like the friendly, hospitable Alice Trout of yesterday.

"Just looking," I said with a smile. "I remember your husband saying a shipment of glassware had come in. Has that been put out yet?"

"Yeah," said Gordon from behind me. "We're looking for some champagne glasses."

Alice glared at Gordon, then shared the unpleasantness with Danny and me. "I don't know if it has," she said. "What you see on the shelves is what's for sale."

"Is your husband around?" Danny asked. "Maybe he'd know."

Alice glowered, looking back and forth between Danny and Gordon as though uncertain where to focus her hostility. "No, he's not around."

"We'll just come back later," I said. "When would be a good time to catch him?"

"He won't be around any time you come here looking for him," said Alice, "and as far as I am concerned, you can all leave right now and never come back. We don't need your kind in Cedar Ridge."

"What kind is that?" I wondered aloud.

"Black, gay, Irish Jews," said Danny. "Cedar Ridge doesn't need 'em."

"Just get out!" Alice fumed. A couple of tourists nearby turned to stare. Alice leaned in close and dropped her voice to a harsh whisper. "Leave my Bert alone!"

"That was one scary woman!" Gordon exclaimed. We were sitting at a table in the Coffee Pot, and a waitress was pouring iced tea all around. Thanks to Alice Trout's abrupt dismissal of our little group, we still had some time before Gordon had to be back at his office. "I'm glad *she* never came after me with an axe handle!"

"From the look on her face, she might yet," Danny remarked. "Was she *born* that belligerent, do you think?"

"No," I told him. "Yesterday she was the very soul of mercantile hospitality." I wondered about Alice's change of heart, and got caught up in my own thoughts, staring into space until Gordon put a hand on my shoulder.

"You still with us?" he asked.

"Oh. Yeah. Just thinking. It's not the easiest thing I do."

Kay Flanders came to the table, looking paler and more nervous than usual. "Would you like to order something to eat?" she asked.

"I was just in here for breakfast," I said, "so I think I'll pass, thanks."

"This is fine for me," Gordon said hoisting his iced tea glass. "As long as I can get a refill or six."

"Me, too," said Danny. "Too early for lunch."

"Oh, well . . . okay, then," Kay said, not moving from the spot.

"Where's Tom gotten himself to?" I asked. "I don't think I've ever sat in here this long without seeing him."

"Oh, he's around someplace, I guess." Kay gestured vaguely at the kitchen and smoking area. She still didn't move.

"I guess he must be awfully busy, huh?"

"Well, Thursday's a busy day," she said, glancing over her shoulder at the doorway into the smoking section. "We have the Business Association meeting at lunchtime, you know."

"No, I didn't know. In this room?"

"There's a meeting room over on the other side," she said, pointing through the doorway to a narrow arch on the far wall of the smoking section that I'd failed to notice on my other visits. "The Business Association meets in there the first Thursday of every month, and this is the first Thursday in July."

"Almost the Fourth," remarked Gordon. "You going to Cedar Meadows for the big fireworks show this year?"

"I really don't know," Kay said absently, her voice trailing off to nothing on the last word. She looked off at the other room for a long moment, then said, "I'll just go get you some more tea."

"Is Kay Flanders always that strange?" I asked.

Danny shrugged. "To tell the truth, I don't eat here all that often. Peter and Cass got into the habit after Tom joined the crusade, but I never cared for the place."

"Me, neither," said Gordon. "All this Southern-style home cooking bothers my stomach."

"Cedar Ridge isn't exactly known for a variety of good

dining-out opportunities," said Danny with a smile. "It's sandwiches, Chinese, Mexican, steak and ribs, and the Aussie's place. If you want anything else, you have to drive to Sacramento or cook it yourself."

"If you can cook," Gordon said to me, "stay and open a restaurant. Please."

"I live alone," I said, holding up a hand in protest. "For me, an elaborate home-cooked meal would be a tuna salad sandwich with green onions *and* water chestnuts. Fortunately, Cascade has a few good restaurants, and a lot more mediocre ones, and I eat out most of the time."

After another glass of iced tea, it was time to return Gordon to his office and Danny to his farmhouse. There was still no sign of Tom.

"Maybe I'll see you at lunchtime," I said to Kay Flanders as we paid our check, and followed it up with a smile—she looked like she needed one.

CHAPTER 20
. . . .

I GAVE PETER A CALL FROM DANNY'S. HE'D BEEN BY Maureen Adler's house, and her trademark pink Caddy was parked in front, but there were no other cars parked anywhere on the lot. He rang the front bell and knocked several times on the door, but no one answered.

A call to Maureen's office brought the information that she had been called away suddenly, and yes, she'd been driving the Caddy. "The thing that bugs me is," said Peter, "if she was in the house, why wouldn't she answer her door, and if she wasn't, where the hell was she?"

"And in what car?" I added. "I guess a car with a few dents in it wouldn't be very incriminating unless the investigation were reopened. If it is, and if that's what she's worried about, she'll have a hell of a time keeping something like that under wraps."

"I found Mark at the video arcade with Robert Terrell," Peter went on, "and he says Dale's pickup was white when he rode in it out to the meeting house, but he also says it was an old paint job. 'Trashed' was the word he used. He couldn't remember one way or another about dents in the right front fender."

I told Peter about our reception at Mountain Arts Collectibles and Treasures, and we agreed it seemed awfully fishy. After hanging up, I stayed for a tour of Danny's garden and two tall glasses of mineral water. It was so peaceful and friendly at Danny's I hated to leave, but eventually I had no other choice.

Armed with a list of Cedar Ridge business people, I drove back to town for a few friendly visits. Some of the people on my list had joined Cass's campaign against the American Rescue Coalition; others had declined to become involved. I had a little rundown on each from my conversations with the gang, and spent the next couple of hours paying calls and finding out nothing I didn't already know. The people who had been scared off were still scared—more so once I had made a connection between the A.R.C.'s death threats and Cass's accident.

The ones who hadn't wanted anything to do with Cass's crusade still didn't, and a few were openly hostile toward her interference after the standard disclaimer about not wanting to speak ill of the dead. No one admitted to having been anywhere near the scene of the accident that Friday night, and none of them did me the favor of incriminating themselves in the least.

What did come out were the feelings that had sundered the community into two camps after the first A.R.C. demonstration. Some people believed Andrew Weiss was a long-overdue American hero; others were equally convinced he was the second coming of Adolf Hitler. Several people told me there'd been groups like this before, deep underground within the community.

No one seemed inclined to name names, and I wasn't in the mood to verbally strong-arm anyone. If it was important, I could always badger them later. While I talked to them, I compared the men's voices with the voices on the videotape, but couldn't make even a tentative match. I noticed that the more businesses I visited, the more people seemed to be expecting me. The grapevine was really humming today. I hoped the vibrations would shake something loose.

I asked casual questions about Maureen Adler until I uncovered the fact that she had an old pink Pinto that she seldom drove anymore. A neighbor of hers who owned and operated a business selling pastel-painted wooden household accessories garnished with bows and dried flowers gave me more information than I wanted about the car. When I expressed an interest in buying it, she informed me that it was in perfect condition as of yesterday morning. Not a scratch on it, and Maureen started it up once a month to keep the battery charged. That seemed to let Maureen off the hook for being somewhere else hiding a car when Peter went by, and perhaps bad manners were all that was needed to explain the rest.

At twelve-fifteen, I weighed my options—lunch or one more call. I was standing outside the Forty-Niner Saloon at the time, and feeling a bit dry. I walked in.

A big man in a white shirt and red suspenders ran a cloth over the antique oak bar with an unmistakably loving touch. "You must own this place," I said, claiming a bar stool near him. Except for a few wilted tourists, the place was deserted.

"Me and the bank," the man acknowledged. "Mostly the bank. You're that detective everybody's talking about, aren't you?" He pulled a Watney's and set it on the bar in front of me.

"I don't know who's talking, but I'm a detective. My name's Caley Burke. How'd you know what I'd order?" I pulled the ice-cold schooner closer.

"It's a hobby of mine. I infer, I contemplate, I deduce. If I'm wrong, I drink it myself." He patted his ample belly. "Took me years to get good at it. I'm Frank Dietrich."

We shook hands. "You were right on the money, Frank. What's the matter, don't I look like the Pink Squirrel type to you?"

Frank Dietrich pulled his head back and squinted expertly at me. "You don't normally drink in the daytime, and you don't drink every day. You came in because it's hotter than the hinge on a whorehouse door out there, and that means you wanted something tall and thirst-quenching, not something sweet and gooey. Besides, you hate gooey drinks."

"You're doing great so far," I acknowledged, taking a swig of the Watney's.

"And you're wearing blue jeans, which the Pink Squirrel ladies are never caught dead in unless they've got some designer's name embroidered on the ass."

"My ass is definitely unembroidered," I agreed. "But why not a Bud?"

"You're not macho enough. You come from out of town, so you might drink some over-advertised import like Heineken, but then there's that air of having lived a little—seen things, done things, you know."

Boy, did I know.

"So the only thing it could be that I've got for sale is a Watney's."

"Frank, you're a genius," I said, finishing the schooner. "I'll have another."

"I guess you're investigating what happened to Cass Lowry," Frank said as he slid the refilled glass to me.

"Is that what 'everyone' is saying?"

"Yep. You have to understand that this town's idea of big news is when the show changes at the El Oro Theater."

Frank took a tray of glasses from beside the sink and turned to put them on a shelf opposite the bar. He watched me in the mirror as he stacked the glasses into a neat pyramid. "Now in a week's time we've had a violent death and a private investigator asking around about it," he said, "and folks can hardly talk about anything else, though if the truth were to be told, none of them know jack shit about it." He finished his pyramid with a flourish and stood back to admire it.

"Nice work," I told him.

"Well, I'm a professional," he said. "You shouldn't expect less."

"Are you from around here, Frank?"

"Originally. I went away for twenty years or so and lived in a lot of other places, first courtesy of the Navy and then just bumming around the world working for a steamship line."

He leaned on the bar and looked around his saloon. "Don't ask me why, but I wanted to own a bar. I came back here for my mother's funeral nine years ago and this place was for sale. I bought it and settled back in like I'd never been gone."

"So I take it you like it here," I said, sipping my second beer a little more slowly than the first.

"Mostly," he said guardedly. He scanned the handful of customers. "Lately there are disturbing elements."

"Minorities?"

"Shit, what's that word mean, anyway? I've been in plenty of places where guys who look like *me* are minorities. There aren't a lot of Caucasians in Nigeria, all things considered. No, the disturbing elements in this town all wear hoods."

"A couple of people have already told me today that people in hoods aren't exactly a new feature around here," I volunteered.

"Yeah, there's always been folks around here that liked to get together in groups to hate their fellow human beings rather than just hating them in solitude. I'll grant you that." He held up a glass to the light coming from behind the liquor bottles and wiped away a water spot. "But I don't think I've ever seen them so ballsy as they've been since they got a dose of Andrew Weiss."

I nodded. My recent dose of Andrew Weiss had made me sick to my stomach. He went down a lot easier with some people around here. "Do you know a local man by the name of Bert Trout?"

Frank laughed. "That little weasel? Yeah, I know him some, but we're not bowling buddies or anything."

"Have you ever thought he might be associated with a group like the American Rescue Coalition?"

"Well, it'd be right up his alley, I can tell you that," he said. He looked at me carefully. "Hell, I can tell you more than that. I've heard him and some of his low-life friends sitting around talking about stuff they were doing for the A.R.C. right here in this bar."

"What kind of stuff?"

"Well, nothing like killing anyone, if that's what you mean, but they talked about a sort of men's club they had that was holding meetings and educating the community about how the poor downtrodden white man was being oppressed, and that kind of shit." He shook his head. "I told them if they were going to sit around and talk like that, they'd better find another place to do it, 'cause I was getting tired of hearing it. Trout hasn't been back since. His wife's one of them, too. The both of them make me more than a little sick, if you want the truth."

I asked Frank for the names of the people he'd seen talking to Bert Trout. A couple of them were business owners I'd talked to today, and one—no surprise—was Dale Reid. The rest were unfamiliar, but maybe Peter and Nora would know the names.

I sighed as I sipped my beer. "This seems like such a nice little town, and then people start telling you about being attacked in parking lots and threats against children. Cass Lowry's dead, and it may not be for any better reason than she got in these people's way."

"It's not the whole town, you know. Everyone's not like them," Frank assured me.

"I know, but I wonder how many of them there are. Is there a critical mass of bigots in a community, and if you reach it the whole place implodes? In a moral sense, of course." I was beginning to feel the beer. Frank was right, I seldom drank in the daytime. When I did, I generally got a little silly and more than a little sleepy.

"I've been all over, Caley," Frank said, "and I've found there's bigotry everywhere you go. This planet has something like five billion people on it and almost all of them think of themselves as belonging to some tribe or other. Little local tribes, tribes the size of whole countries. It's all the same thing."

He poured himself a glass of soda water and emptied it in four long swallows. "When you think like that," he went on, "it's easy to get the idea that the people in your tribe are good and right and the people in the tribe over the hill are evil and wicked and wrong, and probably don't deserve to live. If the people in that other tribe happen to look different than you, or speak a different language, or have different customs or religion, it's all the more excuse to hate them."

"What's the cure, then?" I asked him. I wasn't just being polite—right then I wanted the answer to that question more than just about anything.

"People have to change the way they think," he said. "One person at a time. You can't be responsible for the way some-one else thinks, but you can be a good example for them by letting them know how you feel about things. That's the only way it gets done, whether it's a little one-horse burg like this one or the whole goddamned world—just one person at a time."

I shook my head. "It sounds hopelessly slow." Five billion people, most of whom don't like one another, and for every person who wants to make things better, like Frank Dietrich, there's a Bert Trout out there making them worse. "And then there's Andrew Weiss—how many people does he influence?"

"A lot," Frank acknowledged, "and once someone gets into a group like the A.R.C. and can name names, it's damned hard to get out."

"You mean like peer pressure?"

"I guess that's part of it, but these groups play dirty even with their own. They have ways of keeping people in the fold."

He put down his bar towel and leaned across the bar on his elbows. "I had a guy come in here one night a few months ago, back before those hooded gorillas took to standing around on corners," he said, "and he was sitting right there where you are now, getting shitfaced and talking to me about these local A.R.C. guys and how he'd gotten in before he knew how low they were, and how bad he wanted out and how afraid he was of them."

I shivered in spite of the heat, imagining a man sitting in this same spot, confessing his fears. "Why did he pick you to confess to?" I wondered.

"Well, besides the fact that people like to unload their worst problems and darkest secrets on bartenders, I went to high school with the guy twenty some years ago, and we were pretty good friends at one time.

"He said they'd made it pretty clear to him there was no getting out of this little fraternity except feet first," Frank went on. "He said he was twice as scared once they told him that, because now they knew he had second thoughts and they were watching him all the time. He'd have told me a lot more, but his wife came in, shut him up, pulled him off that bar stool, and dragged him home. I felt so sorry for that sonofabitch, I can't tell you."

I drained the last of the schooner and set it down on the mirror-bright surface of the old bar. "There's one more thing you can do for me, Frank."

"You name it, Caley. Another of those, maybe?"

"No, I think I'd like to be conscious the rest of the day." I got off my bar stool, looked up at the price of the beer, and put twice that onto the counter by the schooner. "I'd just like to know who that was who was talking to you. I swear to whoever you care to name that no one will ever know it was you who told me."

Frank did another quick scan for familiar faces and nodded. "I guess I ought to do what I can to help," he said. "But I've never told this to anyone, and I'm holding you to secrecy. If I get tarred, feathered, and crucified by a bunch of bedsheet-wearing rednecks, I'll come back to haunt you sure as shit."

"It'll be our secret, Frank."

"All right, then. It was a fellow by the name of Tom Flanders. He owns that restaurant up the road a bit on the other side. The Coffee Pot. You know the place?"

I sank back down onto the stool, knees shaking. "Yeah," I said, barely able to breathe. "I know the place."

CHAPTER 21

I NEEDED TO GET THIS NEWS OFF MY CHEST, AND MY CALL TO the Gold Mountain Bookstore was frustrating, netting me a voice-mail message that evidently kicked in when the phone was busy. I called three more times before I gave up.

Peter wasn't answering, which he sometimes didn't when he has working, but I sort of hoped he'd make an exception while I was out gathering vital information for him. Maybe he just wasn't home. Maybe I should calm the hell down. I got back in the car and drove to the *Sentinel*.

"He's at the Business Association meeting," Amanda informed me. "They hold it over at the Coffee Pot the first Thursday of every month."

"Of course." Kay had mentioned the meeting earlier. I should have expected Tim, with his exaggerated sense of civic pride, to be present at this sort of function. "I'm on my way over there anyway," I said, deciding as I spoke, "so I'll see him there." I turned to walk out the door.

"Miss? Wait! Wait, please," Amanda requested.

I stopped and turned back.

"As long as you're going over there, would you mind taking this package? He's been so impatient about it, and he won't be coming back to the office today."

She brought up a parcel, slightly smaller than a breadbox, wrapped in plain brown paper. "It's his Hollywood box—

that's what we call it. He gets a package from down south twice a month and we like to tease him about what might be in it." She turned a delicate shade of rose pink. "There's no end of jokes about it, and some of them quite naughty, as you might imagine. It's all in good fun, though," she added.

"I'm sure it is," I said, taking the box. "I'll be glad to pass it along, and you can be preparing today's jokes before he gets back to the office."

The Thursday lunch meeting of the Cedar Ridge Business Association was well under way when I walked back into the Coffee Pot. Tables were arranged in a large rectangle, with a tabletop podium set up at one place. I saw Dolores and Tim in the crowd. I caught Tim's eye and held up his package. He stared for a moment before nodding recognition. Mike McCutcheon raised a hand in greeting. I waved back automatically, then wished I hadn't.

Tom Flanders was nowhere in sight, but Kay was stationed at the front register. She smiled when she saw me and picked up a menu out of the holder on the side of the register counter. "Just one for lunch?"

I nodded, forcing a smile, and followed her into the non-smoking room. Why had she been acting so strangely this morning? I wondered. Was she looking for an opportunity to tell me something, or just trying to overhear our conversation? I wanted badly to pin her to the wall about Tom and his involvement with the Weiss crowd, but if she was a sympathizer too, or even if she were just afraid for Tom, she'd tip him off immediately. I didn't want that to happen just yet.

I accepted a menu and looked at it without seeing anything. "This is going to take me a few minutes," I said apologetically. "Can you come back?"

"No trouble at all," she said. "Can I bring you some iced tea while you're deciding?"

"That would be good, yes." I watched Kay walk away and looked around for Tom. He was just coming out of the back meeting room. I prayed he wouldn't see me and come over right then—I wasn't certain of my ability to do a creditable job of pretending I thought he was still a good guy. This particular lie would take a little mental preparation, and right now I had to fire up my memory.

This morning Peter and I had discussed Bert Trout in front of Tom. Two hours later, Bert was nowhere to be found when I took Danny and Gordon by the store, and Alice had been openly hostile to us. We had also discussed Maureen Adler, the big real estate deal, and the possibility that she owned a second car. Soon after that she got a phone call at her office and rushed home, but when Peter got there she was either gone in a car other than her Cadillac or pointedly not answering her door. I'd be willing to bet Dale Reid's pickup would also be mighty scarce in the near future.

How many times had I said something in front of Tom Flanders, assuming he was on the same side I was? How many people had he tipped off? How many times had he leaked information to the A.R.C. about Cass and the gang?

I dug out my notebook and went back through the torn-out pages I had stuffed back between the covers, until I found the one I was looking for. Tom Flanders had been at the meeting at Dolores Boyd's house the night Cass died. I needed to find out when he left and when Cass left. Tom was afraid of the A.R.C.—how far would he go because of that fear? As far as killing for them?

Kay came back with my tea, but I couldn't bring myself to eat anything. I handed the menu back with an apology. I still had to impart this news to Nora and Peter, and I wasn't looking forward to it with much enthusiasm. I was staring distractedly at nothing when a figure walked into my field of vision.

"You look deep in thought," said Mike McCutcheon. "Mind if I join you?"

"Well, the thoughts are private, but there's room at the table." I gestured to a chair opposite me.

Mike took the chair beside me and granted me a wide smile full of even white teeth. "Enjoying your vacation?"

"I'm sure you haven't missed the news that I'm not exactly here on a pleasure trip," I said. "It's all over town these days."

"It would be pretty hard to miss that kind of news around here," he agreed. "The problem is, news turns to gossip and gossip becomes wild conjecture. The stories get bigger and harder to believe every day."

"Well, the truth isn't very glamorous," I said. "I'm conducting an investigation into Cassandra Lowry's accident last week. It isn't much like a television show, I'm afraid."

"So how does an investigator go about investigating?" Mike asked. "I confess the only ones I know about are the ones on TV."

It was clear Mike wasn't going to go away and let me put my disjointed thoughts together. I suppressed a sigh. "Well, one thing I did was to go over the official reports, in case there was some evidence that might have been missed or misinterpreted. I've also been talking to a lot of people around town."

Mike snapped his fingers. "I'll bet that's what you were doing over at Kingdom's place yesterday."

"That's right. He was the first person on the scene of the accident, and I wanted to know what he saw—hear it in his own words."

"Who else have you been talking to? Anybody interesting?"

"I just had a beer with Frank Dietrich. He's pretty interesting."

"Good old Frank," Mike said, nodding his head. "We went to school together—he was a couple years ahead of me. He left here to enlist in the Navy just as we were getting out of 'Nam. Missed the whole thing."

"I understand you didn't. Miss it, that is."

"Nope. I was there. But I'm deeply hurt, Caley Burke," Mike said, bowing his head in mock sorrow.

"You are? How did I manage that?"

"You haven't talked to *me* yet." He brightened. "Or maybe you think I'm such a nice guy you can't bear to consider me a suspect."

"I'm sure that's not it, Mike," said Tim Wynand. He pulled out the chair opposite me and sat down. "Hi, Caley."

"Hi, Tim. To knock a hole in your theory, Mike, I've talked to Tim a couple of times and he's not a suspect, either."

"Worse!" Mike cried. "I have competition!"

Tim's eyes twinkled as he looked at me for a long moment. "Maybe you do, Mike. I was just about to ask Caley if she'd join me for dinner tonight."

"Which one of Cedar Ridge's fine dining establishments did you have in mind?" I asked. I remembered Danny's rundown of the pitiful state of local cuisine. "Australian pasta again?"

"I was thinking we'd take a drive out of town. Maybe hit Sacramento for some North Indian food."

Now, that sounded good. And I had to admit to myself that I enjoyed Tim's company. Too bad I had other plans.

"Can I get a rain check on that offer?" I asked him. "I'm really going to need to do some work on this case tonight."

Tim's eyes widened with interest. "Things heating up a bit?"

"Just a bit. It's nothing I can talk about now, but I should stay on top of it."

Tim touched my hand. "We'll do it when you're free, then." He got up from the table and pushed his chair back in. "Looks like we're both out of luck for now, Mikey."

"Oh, don't forget your package," I reminded him. I picked it up from the chair where I'd left it and handed it to him.

"Thanks, Caley," he said, tucking the parcel under one arm. "See you around."

Mike watched Tim walk away, then turned back to me. "So I guess you're not interested in a guided tour of the hot spots of Cedar Ridge?"

"Right now, they're *all* hot. But since you know more about this town than practically anyone," I said, "maybe there's something you could help me with."

"Name it." He spread his hands wide in a gesture of unlimited generosity.

"There's a big real-estate deal cooking around here—what do you know about it?"

"Well, Cedar Ridge real estate is pretty healthy right now, compared to the rest of the state, so there's a lot of activity in general."

"No, I mean something really big. Millions and millions."

"That would have to be the hotel deal," said Mike. "Maureen Adler got her hooks into some Sacramento investors and they're cooking up a sale to one of the big hotel chains—whichever one wants to pay the most for it. They've been buying up all the land on that corner for good prices and getting ready to make a killing."

"Maureen seems to place quite a lot of importance on the deal going through. I talked with her yesterday about it, and she was downright agitated at the thought something might go wrong."

Mike shrugged. "Well, the hotel would be a good thing for the town—I confess I'm in favor of it. And you've got to figure she's taking some kind of commission on the sale. Even a finder's fee would be pretty substantial, and if I know Maureen, she held out for all she could get."

"I wonder," I muttered aloud.

"Aw, come on. Don't tell me Maureen's a suspect and I'm still just the nice guy who owns the car lot. I thought I'd have something to tell my grandkids."

"Sorry," I said, getting up and leaving money on the table. "If you want me to pay attention to you, you'll have to incriminate yourself. See you around, Mike."

My next stop was supposed to be the bookstore—I needed to let Nora in on today's developments. My plans were suddenly changed when I pulled out of the Coffee Pot's parking lot and a white sheriff's sedan that had been parked facing the road with its motor running pulled out in front of me. The driver looked into the rearview to make sure I was tailing. Now this was a switch. Instead of following, Deputy Judy Roy was now leading me. I decided to go along for the ride.

She drove all the way through town and back out the south end, then turned east and headed higher into the Sierra Nevada foothills. I kept a cautious distance between us as the road wound nauseatingly around the side of a mountain, and tried not to glance down at the drop-off that seemed to go down forever. The flimsy guardrails that flanked the road didn't serve to reassure me of my safety.

We passed through a little mountain town and kept going. About ten miles on the other side, a small cafe appeared on the side of the road, and the white sedan pulled in. I parked a few feet away. This time I got out of my car. If this was going to be another threat, I wanted to face it standing up.

Judy Roy got out of her car. "Let's go inside," she said.

We sat down at a booth by a window. A waitress in pink nylon took our orders: iced tea for me and coffee for Judy. A ceiling fan moved warm air around with a labored sound.

"You're probably wondering what the hell this is all about," said Judy. She took off her hat and set it down on the table. Her hair was corralled on top of her head, but some of it was starting to fall down in little sweaty tendrils along her neck.

"That's a pretty safe guess," I said. "What *is* this all about?" I'd been verbally muscled once this week, and I wasn't in the mood to take any more abuse gracefully.

"Until about three months ago, I used to go out with Craig Bellenger," she said.

It would be rude to make a remark about her taste in men, however grouchy I might be feeling. I just nodded.

"We were a pretty serious item, but the Department has a rule against deputies cohabiting, and I wasn't ready to get married. I'm glad I wasn't, because Craig was always trying to talk me into it." Our drinks came, and we busied ourselves self-consciously with doctoring them.

"At some point," Judy went on, "he started trusting me. He started telling me things he thought I should know about him."

"Things like what?" I inquired.

"There's this meeting he went to every Thursday night—the Men's Club, he called it. I used to ask him what they did there, but he was pretty cagey about it. He'd say it was just a social group, and the next time I asked he said they raised money for political causes, but he wouldn't say which ones. Personally, I figured they must be getting together to watch porno tapes or something. After a while I quit asking because the whole subject bugged the shit out of me." She stirred two sugars into her coffee, evidently forgetting she had put two in a minute ago.

"So when he decided to tell me everything about himself, he told me about the Men's Club." She took a drink of the coffee and grimaced.

I waited a few seconds, then prompted her. "What did he tell you?"

She looked at me, then down at her cup. "It's a chapter of the American Rescue Coalition."

The news of Craig Bellenger's affiliation with Andrew Weiss's white supremacist organization wasn't nearly as much of a shock to me as it must have been to Judy at the time. Even remembering it seemed to make her feel ill. Her face had lost a lot of color and her hand trembled on the handle of the coffee cup. I put out a hand and squeezed hers. She smiled weakly.

"Do you know anybody else who was involved?"

"He mentioned a couple of people in the Department, Johnny Hughson and somebody named Jim Lauderdale. Hughson's a local boy who's been with the Sheriff's Department eight or ten years. Lauderdale was stationed at the other end of the county, and I never met him. I think he was higher in rank, the way Craig talked about him."

"Did he mention any other names?" I asked.

"Other than those, no. I think he told me about the guys in the Department because he wanted me to think it was legitimate in some way." She shuddered. "As if I ever could. It goes to show how little he knew me."

"And maybe how little you knew him," I suggested. "Do you know where they meet?"

"If I did, I'd probably burn the place down some Thursday night when they were all inside. I should have followed him there."

"It's a good thing you didn't," I said. "You're lousy at it."

She laughed at that. "I hoped you'd notice. There was no way I could chance being seen talking to you in town. Being conspicuous enough to get you curious seemed like the best plan."

"Well, it worked. And it's Thursday, isn't it? I think I'm losing track."

"You don't mean you're going to try to find the meeting!"

"It's that or wait until next week. By next week this time I want to be home drinking an iced latte."

"These guys are dangerous," Judy said.

"Dangerous enough to kill someone?"

"You mean Cassandra Lowry?"

"She got in their faces and she's dead," I said. "There's no proof, of course . . ."

"But there could be," Judy said, looking thoughtful. "If we could find out where they're meeting, we might be able to learn any number of things."

"Was that a *we* I heard? This probably isn't something you should be involved in," I cautioned her. "If something went wrong, you could be jeopardizing your career. As it is, I may decide to use the names you gave me as bait. What happens if Craig figures you for my source of information?"

"I know the risks better than you do," she told me. "I want to clear out this nest of slugs. Craig never does anything without shooting off his mouth about it first."

"And having shot off, does he follow through?" I couldn't help thinking about his thinly veiled threats of the previous day.

"Always."

"Then you have to promise me that if he threatens you, you'll get the hell out of his way until he's behind bars."

"I will," she said, "but first I want to help put him there." I searched her eyes. They were calm and determined, but the tension in her body betrayed a certain eagerness.

"Off duty, out of uniform?"

"Until I know who we can trust, yes. Now how do you figure to find the place?"

"Leave it to me," I told her. "I know someone who knows the way."

CHAPTER 22

NORA WAS IN SACRAMENTO AT THE PAPERBACK WAREHOUSE when I tried to call her at the bookstore from the pay phone outside the coffee shop. Judy had pulled off ahead of me and I'd decided it might be best if we weren't seen driving back into town together, so I dug out some dimes and made my calls.

I was afraid to leave Nora too specific a message for fear someone working at the store might be a friend or relation to Tom Flanders, so I just said something to the effect that future meetings would not take place at the Coffee Pot, and hoped that would be enough until I could talk to her in person.

Peter wasn't answering the phone at the house, so I left him a more specific message. I told him everything Frank Dietrich had told me, and to get hold of Dolores and Danny and for all of them to try to remember everything that had ever been said in front of Tom Flanders. The only possible damage control I could imagine now, I said, was to make sure Flanders never heard anything useful again.

At the end of the message I trailed off, saying goodbye in about five times as many words as necessary. I get flustered if I have to talk too long into an answering machine, because they never give you any conversational feedback. Toward the end of any message longer than a few words I start repeating myself, and I'm never sure how to wrap up the one-sided conversation. If it weren't for how much I love my computer, I'd be convinced I wasn't meant to live in the communications age.

I half expected to see the man in the blue sedan pulling out from the coffee shop behind me, but he apparently hadn't come along on this trip. I almost missed him, but not quite. Someone was keeping an eye on me, but you'd think with Tom Flanders overhearing every detail of the investigation so far, there'd be no need to go to so much trouble. Maybe they just didn't trust Tom enough to let him do his job.

On the way back into town I passed the Forest Service station again. Smokey the Bear stood outside on the Fire Danger sign, shovel at the ready. The sign now proclaimed "Fire Danger: Extreme." I could believe it. The dry grasses on the hillsides looked ready to burst into flame from the touch of the pitiless July sun. The sky was a violent shade of blue, crackling with heat, and a hot, dry wind threw up dust devils on the side of the road.

I was almost past the station when I spotted Eddie Shepard wearing an olive-drab coverall and washing a yellow-green fire engine that was pulled up onto a gravel driveway next to the main building. The station doors were open and no other trucks were in evidence. I braked and pulled up beside him. "You minding the store?" I asked as I rolled down my window.

Eddie turned around and looked at me, carefully keeping the hose trained on the fire truck. "Oh, hi." The permanent frown lines between his eyes deepened just a bit. "Yeah, there's a grasser a few miles south of town, and Dale Reid's crew drew the short straw."

"Grass fire?"

"Yeah. Probably some moron tossing a cigarette butt, or kids with firecrackers." He turned back to the fire engine and picked up a squirt bottle of solvent, which he sprayed onto a tar spot. "Tomorrow's the Fourth, and we usually get a little one or two around this time every year."

"Where I live, fireworks are illegal."

Eddie snorted. "They're illegal here, too, but dealers bring them in from Mexico, and if you know who to ask, you can always get ahold of some."

"It's a bad day for it," I commented. "It's even getting a little windy."

"Oh, I don't imagine it amounts to much. They'll have it under control and be back here before you can write home to Mother." He massaged the tar spot with a sponge and aimed a jet of water at it, most of which bounced back and covered him in a fine mist.

"That looks like the coolest work you can get around this place," I commented.

Eddie nodded. "Yeah, at least this way I can get some water on me."

"Didn't you always love to play in the sprinkler when you were little?" I asked. "No one lets you do that when you grow up. That must be why adults like to wash their cars."

"I don't know about that," Eddie replied, aiming a burst of spray at the rear tire of the truck, "Not much use washing my car when I'm going up and down a dirt road every morning and night, but if the Federal Government wants to pay me by the hour to hose myself down on a day like this, I'm taking it."

I got out of the car and sat up on the front fender. "Speaking of kids, yours are sure growing up, aren't they?"

Eddie smiled, an uncommon expression for him. "They'll be in school this fall," he said. "I remember when they were so little I could hold both of them at one time. One in each arm." His free arm crooked reflexively as if it could remember the feeling of holding an infant son. Whatever Eddie's faults, he had a genuine soft spot for Matt and Harry.

"They're great kids." I waited while Eddie nodded assent to this. "Nora says you haven't seen them since the last weekend in May. It's July now, you know."

He turned his head to frown at me. "I've been busy. And I don't think it's any of your business, anyway."

"You're right. It isn't, really." There was a thin paperback book sticking out of his back pocket. I've always been insatiably curious about what other people are reading, and I wanted to see if I could tweak Eddie a bit, anyway. I reached out and snatched the book. He turned and made a grab for it, and I ducked under a spray of water.

"Hold it, Eddie! I'll give it back—I just wanted to see what was so interesting that it could induce you to read." I looked at the cover. An American flag rippled in the background with the title in bold black letters superimposed on it. Recognizing the book only made my stomach twist a little—I must be getting used to this shit, I thought. "*Let's Bring Back America*, by Andrew Weiss. I don't think I've read this one. What's it about?"

Eddie turned off the hose and faced me. "It's about how to make this country great again," he said evenly. "It's about how guys like me can help America be a place we'll be proud to raise our children in. Have you got a problem with that?"

"Not in theory," I admitted. "Not when it's put in such glowing generalities. I mean, who can object to images of Mom, home, and apple pie? It's the way the generalities are put into practice that frightens me." I handed the book back.

"What do you mean?" he asked, taking it in his free hand. He turned the hose back on and rinsed detergent from the back of the truck.

"Like putting on hoods and beating up your neighbors; promoting hate and separatism as a remedy for problems caused by hate and separatism; standing around on street corners looking like a casting call for *Birth of a Nation*. That sort of thing."

Eddie's look grew sullen. "I don't know what the fuck you're talking about."

"I think maybe you do. I think you're either a part of the local A.R.C. or a major sympathizer. Don't feel lonely, though. I think that about a number of folks around town right now. It doesn't mean I believe you had anything to do with what happened to Cass."

Eddie let the hose angle down, gripping it until his knuckles turned white. I was getting to him. Good.

"Nothing happened to Cass but a goddamned car wreck. And you don't understand anything that's going on here." The water from the hose sluiced over Eddie's shoes and cut a hole through the gravel into the sandy dirt under his feet. "You don't know what's at stake."

I pointed to the book in his hand. "I was lying when I said I haven't read it," I told him. "I know what's in there, cover to cover."

The look on his face told me how much that surprised him. "What did you think?" he asked. His expression was curious, almost friendly.

"I think I find his kind of politics revolting and detestable."

"Andrew Weiss isn't about politics, Caley," Eddie protested, shaking the book in my face. "You read him, but you don't understand. He's about information—things we need to know. This book tells about the takeover that's going on in our country and how to stop it—how to bring America back."

"Eddie, Andrew Weiss is a man sick with hate who has a pretty farfetched vision of what America should be like. A better word for it might be 'delusion.' You and your hooded buddies are trying to shape your community and your country around a lunatic's delusion."

"The America Andrew Weiss wants to bring back is the America that was always meant to be," he shot back. "Niggers and Jews and queers and Communists weren't meant to run this country. *We* were."

He gestured out into the wide world in general, warming to his topic. "All those spics and Chinks and dog-eating gooks who come here and don't even bother to learn our language shouldn't be voting and making laws. *We* should. White people. People like you and me."

I bristled. "Don't lump me in with your pure white nation, Eddie. It's not the America I live in, and it never was. You honestly believe you'd want to raise your children in a country like the one Andrew Weiss describes in that book?"

"My children . . ." Eddie sputtered. "My children have a right to live in a free country." Tears sprang into his eyes and he wiped at them with the sleeve of the coveralls. "You're just like Nora and Cass—blind to what's really happening in this country. And Nora wants to raise my boys blind, too. It's not her fault, I know. That lesbo-feminist Commie mother of hers turned Nora into another one just like her, and I couldn't do anything to stop her."

"My children . . ." Eddie had said. "My children . . ." the otherwise silent man in the videotape had begun to protest. I compared the two in my mind and added the expression on Cass's face when she realized who she was talking to— her ex–son-in-law. I sat back on my car fender to conceal the shaking in my legs.

"You really hated Cass, didn't you?" I said when I could talk again.

Eddie stiffened and the tears stopped. "I guess I did for a while, but I'd never hurt her or anything if that's what you're getting at."

"Well, that *is* the reason I'm in town. I guess you know that by now."

"I'd have to be pretty stupid not to."

I decided to spare Eddie my evaluation of his intelligence. "Do you know anything about what happened to Cass last Thursday night that might not be in the official reports?" I asked him point-blank. "Someone killed Cass Lowry. It may have been one of your good buddies in the hoods. Is there anything you'd like to say about that?"

"I think you're asking the wrong guy if you think someone killed Cass. I didn't hate her anymore, and Nora was never coming back to me anyway, and hurting Cass couldn't do anything for me." Eddie seemed to notice the hose and switched it off again.

"But it might have been helpful to someone you know," I pressed.

"You're crazy. Sure, I know guys who are A.R.C., and they were plenty pissed at Cass, but they'd never kill a woman."

"Does that mean they *would* kill a man? If Danny Abrahams and Gordon Terrell hadn't fought back, would they be dead now, too?"

Eddie's frown invaded his entire face, jaw clenched tight, lips compressed to a tense line. "I don't know anything about anybody getting beat up."

"I didn't say they were."

"It's not a secret. I hear stuff around town, and I see Nora every two weeks. We talk."

"You didn't pick up the boys the weekend of the last A.R.C. rally. You told Nora you had something important to do. Something like carrying a placard and passing out pamphlets?"

"Something like none of your fucking business," he replied.

I held up my hands in a gesture of defeat. "You got me again. Unfortunately, my business consists of finding out things that are none of my fucking business. That's how I earn my living."

"You can dig as deep as you want to, and you won't find anything you haven't already," Eddie said. He reached around and put the book into his back pocket. "Nobody killed Cass except her own carelessness on a bad old mountain road."

"I want you to think about some things, Eddie. Cass went off the side of a road she could drive in her sleep. The moon was up and the night was clear and the road was dry. She'd recognized someone under one of those hoods the weekend before, and she'd received death threats, which she blatantly ignored." I watched him as I spoke. All this thinking was hard on him, and the mention of Cass and the A.R.C. rally had made him go pale. This was no time to let up.

"Kingdom Neary called an ambulance when he got to the scene, and it arrived in five minutes, which it couldn't do unless it was clocking over a hundred on those nasty turns going up Black Mountain Road. The sheriff's deputies got there even sooner. Now, how'd they know there'd been an accident before anyone got there?"

Eddie didn't volunteer an answer.

"Dale Reid drives a white pickup truck," I continued. "That's the same color as Cass's car in case you've forgotten. Some time in the very recent past he got a new paint job. A bad, amateurish, hurry-up paint job that didn't do much for the dents in his right front fender."

I was rolling, and it took fast thinking to omit information that shouldn't be given to Eddie, like the fact that I was on to Tom Flanders. "I don't believe Cass's death was an accident, Eddie, and if you think about it very hard, you won't either. It's possible your friends neglected to inform you that they killed your ex-wife's mother; you might want to jog their manners a bit."

I walked around to face him as he tried to turn away from me. "I never thought of you as the type who went in for murder, but someone in this town does, and I think you know who it is, and I don't think you want to go down with them when they go. And they will go, Eddie. Trust me on this one."

"I wouldn't ever have killed Cass," Eddie said, shaking his head. "I never liked her much, I'll admit that. Nora wasn't raised right and that was Cass's fault," he said, a mournful expression beginning to replace the trademark frown. "Cass got Nora to leave me and she even got her to leave my name. That's when I knew Nora wasn't ever coming back, when she gave up the name I gave her. Now all I've got is my boys, and I hope they'll understand what I'm doing, 'cause I'm doing it for them."

Eddie switched the hose back on and resumed washing the fire engine. "You read the book again, Caley," he said over his shoulder. "And this time you pay attention to what Andrew Weiss is saying, or you're going to wake up and find your country's been taken away from you."

"Why don't you go by and see your boys tonight, Eddie? Even if you're still too busy to take them for the weekend, just go by the house and spend a little time with them. And while you're there, think about whether you want them to grow up to be like your friends—the ones who murdered their grandmother."

CHAPTER 23

DOLORES BOYD'S BUSINESS, THE ANTIQUE BARN, WAS NEAR the center of town about half a block from the Coffee Cup. I stood outside and checked out the view for a moment before going in. To the south, the air had taken on a sickly yellow-gray cast—smoke from the grass fire Eddie had talked about, no doubt. Sweat was already starting to trickle down my neck by the time I pushed the door open and felt the pleasant rush of cool air from inside.

A bell chimed and Dolores looked up from a case of antique jewelry she was rearranging and smiled broadly when she saw me. "Oh, Caley, it's good to see you!" she exclaimed. She executed an expert turn in the narrow space between two display cases and rolled over to me.

"I'm not sure how happy you're going to be when I fill you in on today's revelations," I said. "Can you get away for a minute?" I indicated the handful of browsers looking over the abundant stock of old furniture, glassware, and rusty kitchen utensils.

"Sure can. I've got a clerk unpacking crates in the back— I'll just call her out here. Shall we go across the street for a cold drink?"

"No." That had come out too abruptly. I laid a reassuring hand on Dolores's shoulder. "Let's just go into the back. Is there someplace we can sit and talk?"

Dolores patted her chair fondly. "I've *always* got a place to sit. We'll see what we can rustle up for you."

Dolores exchanged places with the clerk and we sat in the combination storage room and office. I sat down in a comfortable club chair opposite a desk piled high with paperwork. I tried leaning back in the chair, but I was too anxious. I scooted forward and sat on the edge of the seat.

Dolores brought two cans of cold fruit punch out of a little refrigerator near her desk and gave one to me. "Now, what's all this about, Caley?" she said, rolling herself to a position beside the desk. "I get the feeling something big is up."

"Tom Flanders was one of the people at the meeting at your house the night Cass was killed. Is that right?"

"Yes," Dolores answered. She cocked her head at me, but I wasn't answering questions right now, I was asking them.

"When did he leave your house? Relative to the time Cass left, I mean."

"He and Nora and Danny were still there when Cass left. Peter hadn't been able to attend because of a deadline he'd been goofing off on all week, so Cass came by herself. Usually the core group stayed around after everyone else had gone home."

"Did that usually include Tom?"

"No, not usually, but that night he seemed sort of depressed, and didn't want to go home right away. He said it was some kind of fuss he was having with Kay. Cass ended up leaving before he did—she'd been awfully tense since the demonstration the weekend before. Nora told me she hadn't been sleeping much, but no one knew exactly what was bothering her. What's this leading up to, anyway?"

"In a minute. So Cass got in her car to drive home. How long after did Tom leave?"

"Let me think. It wasn't more than a couple of minutes, I guess. He got up to go right after Cass walked out the door; then he asked if he could make a phone call."

"Did you hear who he was talking to or anything he said?"

"He went in the other room and used the phone," said Dolores. "Then he said good night and drove off."

"What was he driving?"

"His pickup—the one he uses for restaurant business. It's some kind of American-made mini-truck."

"Color?"

"Red. Caley, you're driving an old woman batshit. What the hell's going on here?"

There was no gentle way of putting it, so I just came out and said it: "Tom Flanders is part of the local A.R.C."

Dolores recoiled as if physically struck. "Tom? Do you have proof?"

"He opened up to someone when he was drunk. Apparently he wanted out before this street corner business started, and was told there wasn't any getting out."

"You trust the person who told you this, don't you," she said, more a confirmation than a question.

I thought about my conversation with Frank Dietrich. I'd been fooled before, but I had a good feeling about Frank. "Yes," I said.

"And you're protecting your source?"

"Wouldn't you?"

Dolores nodded. "Do you think Tom had anything to do with . . ."

"It's possible. If he didn't, I'd at least be willing to bet he called and told someone she was coming their way." I related what Frank had said about Tom wanting out of the A.R.C., and being afraid of them. "I think when Cass announced a meeting about the first demonstration, they planted Tom in the group as a source of information. Anything anyone's ever said in front of him probably went right back to whoever's running the local organization."

"Christ on a bender," said Dolores, shaking her head. "We've all talked in front of Tom constantly, from the very beginning. He was so eager to join up and be a part of everything that was going on."

"Yes, he's been especially keen on letting me know how much a part of the group he was," I said, thinking back on previous talks with Tom. "Today I started noticing how information's been getting out. Tom knew I was going to Sacramento yesterday. Some psycho driver who may have been Dale Reid got crazy with me on the way back, and

Craig Bellenger stopped me and gave me a rather menacing safety lecture."

"Yes, Nora told me about that," said Dolores.

"Tom knew I was taking Danny and Gordon to possibly ID Bert Trout. When we got there, Bert was history, and Alice treated us like an infestation of head lice. Tom knew Cass was on her way home alone in her car, and she never got there."

We were both silent for half a minute; then Dolores spoke up.

"Now what do we do?"

I shrugged. "We keep on giving him information."

"Are you nuts?" Her expression told me she was pretty certain of the diagnosis.

"Possibly, but there's a method to it. Let's leak something and follow it where it goes."

"Such as what?"

"Such as the fact that we know Craig Bellenger and two other deputies we can name are part of the A.R.C."

"Isn't that a bit risky? What if it's not true? It could backfire on us something fierce."

"It's true," I said. "I've got it on very good authority. And that's not even the worst of it."

"I'm going to be sorry I asked, but what's the worst?"

"Eddie Shepard's one of them, too."

Dolores's face fell even further. "Oh, Caley. Are you absolutely sure?"

"Yes. Cass recognized him at the second demonstration. She must not have known how to break it to Nora, so she hadn't said anything yet when she died."

"Poor Nora."

I nodded. "This is going to be hard on her, especially now, and especially if Eddie turns out to be implicated in Cass's death.

"You remember it was pretty common practice to threaten the children of people who supported the gang if milder threats didn't have any effect. Did anyone ever notice that Nora never received any threats against her children?"

"Oh, my goodness, no," said Dolores. "We were paying so much attention to what was going on, we didn't have any brain cells to spare for what *wasn't*. It makes sense, though. Eddie's always been so protective of those boys. If he was part of it, and his cronies had tried anything like that, he'd have gone berserk for sure."

"He was part of it, all right," I assured her.

I checked the time on Mickey and got up. "Sorry to dump on you and run, but I have a busy night ahead of me and I have to contact some people."

"That's quite all right, dear. I'm as tough an old bird as you're ever likely to meet, and if I can handle all the shit that's come to pass around here so far, I can handle whatever's to come."

"I'm glad you feel that way," I told her. "I'm going to need someone to help me pull this thing off in front of Tom, and I don't think Peter and Nora will be able to carry off the act. Would you like to have dinner with me after you close this place?"

Dolores looked up at me with a kind of sad determination. "Six-thirty at the Coffee Cup?"

"It's a date."

I called the number Mark Birdsall had given me and asked if he wanted to go for a drive this evening.

"Time to scope out the Nazi bungalow, huh?"

"That's right. I'll have a friend with me—someone we can trust. I want you to find the meeting house for us."

"I don't have any hot dates I have to break," he said. "Pick me up whenever."

"Whenever should be around eight. That will give us a little daylight to play with while you find the place. Wear something dark."

"You forget I'm a metalhead," he said with a good-natured laugh. "Everything in my closet is black."

I picked up the man in the dark blue sedan again as I pulled away from the phone booth. He might have been around since I left the Antique Barn, but I'd been too fried to notice. How was I going to make a secret trip to the meeting house with this guy turning up everywhere? I pulled over to a wide spot on the side of the road and let the cars behind me pass, including the blue sedan. I could swear I saw a wry smile on his face as he drove by.

Tim Wynand was putting his package into the trunk of his car when I drove past the *Foothills Sentinel* building. On impulse, I turned into the driveway and greeted him.

"I thought you weren't coming back here today," I said.

He gave me a delighted smile. "I wasn't planning to, but now I'm glad I did. Change your mind about dinner in Sacramento?" He closed and locked the trunk.

"I wish I could. Things are breaking, and I don't know when I'll have a spare minute."

"Want to talk about it? I was just taking off for a walk in the park. I do it every day about this time. You could join me."

I thought about time and decided I could spare a few minutes to update Tim on the case. He had an interest in the outcome, and he'd gone out of his way to get information I wanted. I'd already armored myself with heavy-duty sunscreen, so I parked my car and we walked a block to the park.

"You do this regardless of weather?" I asked, the mid-afternoon heat seeming to sink through my skin and cook me inside and out.

"Unless it rains, which it doesn't do all that often in this part of the state nine months of the year. The secret to getting along with heat is not to fight it. If you tense up, resist the heat, it makes you feel hotter. Just relax and experience it as part of what's going on—let it pass through you. Try it."

I looked at Tim, cool as a cucumber in a crisp white shirt. It seemed to work for him, I noted. What did I have to lose? I relaxed and let myself accept the heat for what it was—an outside condition. I ceased resisting it and accepted it on its own terms. As soon as I did, I began to feel cooler and more energetic. I looked over at Tim. "Hey, it works!"

"Of course it works." His blue eyes twinkled. "I'd never steer you wrong, Caley." He put an arm across my shoulders. "So what's up that's so important you couldn't get away tonight?"

"So much I don't know how to handle it all in one night. For starters, the A.R.C. planted an observer in Cass's group."

"That doesn't surprise me—they would have felt threatened by what she was doing. Who was it?"

"Tom Flanders. He joined up at the first meeting, and hung around as much as possible to get the skinny on what the group knew and what they were doing. He must have known the TV crew was coming, and he certainly knew when Cass left Dolores's house on the night she was killed, and that she was alone in the car."

Tim's face went pale. "Hold it," he said, bringing me up short with a hand on my arm. "Do you have proof of any of this?"

"I have proof he's part of the A.R.C. I also know when they hold their meetings, and tonight I'm going to find out where." I walked out of his grip and continued on. "There are some other things you don't know or haven't considered," I continued. I proceeded to lay out the facts as I had outlined them to Eddie shortly before—Kingdom Neary and the ambulance and the sheriff's cars, Dale Reid and his hastily painted pickup. For good measure I threw in Tom Flanders's conveniently timed phone call the night of Cass's death and the fact that she'd ID'd Eddie at the demonstration.

When I was through spouting off, I turned and looked at him. His face was white and strained.

We arrived at the park and walked across a wide expanse of sunburnt grass in silence. Tim pointed out a bench on the far side, shaded by trees. "Let's talk over there," he suggested. We crossed the park to the bench and sat down.

"Caley, I know I'm the one who's been saying this murder theory is farfetched," he said, "but you've convinced me there might be something to it. If the people you're talking about killed Cass—" Here his voice broke, and he had to look away for a moment before he could go on. "If they did, then they might not stop at killing again. I don't want you to do anything that might be dangerous."

"I'm being paid to get facts," I reminded him. "I'm not going to deliberately endanger myself if I can help it, but on the other hand I can't just walk up to Tom Flanders and ask him to tell me everything he knows."

"You could call the Sheriff's Department. Maybe they'd send someone with you."

I sighed. "First, that's not the way they operate. Second, I'm going to be guilty of trespassing at best, and breaking and entering at worst. They don't take that sort of thing well."

"You're not going in there!"

"Not if anyone's in the house, but if they've moved the meeting and the place looks deserted, I'll go in and have a look. I'd be crazy not to. And third, Tim, some of the sheriff's deputies are part of it, too."

"This is totally insane."

"Hey, you're the one who didn't believe they killed anyone, right?"

Tim's face hardened. "For their sakes, they better not have."

I put a hand on his arm. "They'll get what's coming to them if we can get enough evidence to get the official investigation reopened. That's what I'm doing here."

"Do you carry a gun?" Tim asked.

I thought of the Walther PP in my trunk—the weapon I'd refused to carry since the night I'd killed for the first time. My mind and body cringed at the thought of picking it up again. "No," I said. "I don't."

"Let me give you one to take with you," he said. "You'll be safer if you have something to defend yourself with."

"I couldn't," I said. "I can't explain why right now, but I just couldn't handle it."

"It would be so . . . awful if something happened to you, too." Tim stopped talking. The muscles in his jaw were knotted and his eyes burned with emotion.

"Nothing's going to happen," I assured him. While I was at it, I assured myself, too. This was going to be a simple walk in the country, with a little eavesdropping thrown in for good measure, just like I told Tim. I had left out some details, like Craig Bellenger's threats and the hatchet-faced man who seemed to turn up everywhere I went. No sense worrying about petty details. "I'll be careful," I said.

CHAPTER 24

I TRIED AGAIN TO REACH NORA AND PETER, BUT WAS ONLY able to leave messages. I told them I'd be out for a few hours, but didn't go into detail—there was no sense in having everyone worried about my safety.

I needed to change for the evening's activities, but going back to the house was out; I didn't want to run into Nora and Peter and have to lie to them. Instead, I visited Cedar Ridge's clothing boutiques until I found what I was looking for among all the brightly colored vacation clothes.

The clerk, who was wearing an orange silk sleeveless top and matching shorts, grimaced when I brought my purchase to the counter. It was a man's shirt, black, long-sleeved, and several sizes too large for me, but its value as camouflage outweighed its lack of fashion merit. I endured her silent judgment and paid my money. As I came out, I noticed the yellow cast in the air had grown more pronounced, and the scent of smoke could be detected in the air. Maybe this grasser had been a little harder to stomp out than Eddie had anticipated.

Dolores and I met at the Coffee Cup as planned, and weren't surprised to see Tom Flanders hurrying over to our table to take our order. He hovered over the table as always, refilling water and coffee and making himself generally convenient to hear our discussion.

"I have the names of three sheriff's deputies who are definitely involved in the American Rescue Coalition," I told Dolores.

She feigned surprise. "That's just awful!" she said.

"Awful!" echoed Tom. "You say you have names?"

I nodded and ticked them off on my fingers. "Craig Bellenger, Johnny Hughson, and Jim Lauderdale. Lauderdale doesn't work out of the Cedar Ridge station anymore, but he's still with the department as far as I know."

"But you don't have proof they had anything to do with what happened to Cass, do you?" Tom asked.

"Not yet. I'm getting closer, though. I don't have enough resources to have them followed, but I'm gathering new evidence all the time."

"That must mean you're just about ready to crack this thing," said Dolores on cue.

"I think by this time tomorrow I'll know who was driving the car that ran Cass off the road, and who gave the order to do it. There'll be another investigation and a lot of people will go to jail, not to mention the shit hitting the fan in the Sheriff's Department." I smiled up at Tom.

Tom let out a breath. "I'll be go to hell!" he exclaimed. His hands, I noted, were trembling more than a little. "If you ladies are fine here for now, I'd better be getting back to the kitchen," he said and hurried off without waiting for confirmation.

From where I was sitting, I couldn't see the kitchen, but Dolores watched Tom's progress out of the corner of her eye and reported it to me. "He's going in the kitchen. Now he's coming back out again, looking around. He's going back to his office."

"Probably to make a phone call," I said. "I think we did a pretty good night's work here."

Kay Flanders appeared at my elbow with a carafe of coffee. "He's a good man," she said in a voice too low for anyone but me to hear as she bent over to refill my cup. "He doesn't always do good things, but he's a good man. Please remember that." Before I could think what to reply, she had walked away again.

● ● ●

I met Judy Roy at a prearranged spot on a county road
west of the highway, and we ditched my white rental Chevy
well off the side of the road. We drove Judy's gray Toyota to
pick up Mark Birdsall at eight—it was just the right color to
disappear into shadow when you turned off the headlights.

Mark was waiting for us on his front porch, dressed in
black jeans and a black T-shirt with dark gray skulls covering
every inch of fabric. "How do you like my Ninja get-up?" he
inquired as he got into the Toyota's back seat.

"Very effective," said Judy, looking him over in the rearview
mirror. "But your hair practically glows in the dark." Judy's
hair was pulled up under a dark watch cap, with only some
wisps of bangs showing on her forehead.

"No problem," said Mark. He pulled a black Raiders ball
cap out of his back pocket and tucked his long blond hair
inside. "Better?"

"Mark, this is Judy," I said by way of introduction. "Judy,
Mark."

"Hey!" said Mark, moving around to get a better look at
Judy. "Aren't you a . . ."

"Not tonight," she replied calmly. "Now, which way do
we go?"

We found the road heading east that Mark remembered
having traveled the night he saw the house with the A.R.C.
posters. I turned and watched the back window for signs of
anyone following us, but the cars that occasionally turned off
of side roads and stayed behind us for a while always turned
into other roads or driveways. Maybe my sinister man had
another engagement tonight. If he was part of the A.R.C., he
might even be at the very place we were heading for.

Now and then Mark would ask Judy to turn in one direction
or another, peering out his window to look at landmarks. I
tried to memorize the route in my head, repeating each turn
over and over to myself. Finally he said, "We're getting close.
It's just up the road."

Judy pulled the car a hundred feet off the road into a
stand of pines and firs, and we started walking. It was completely dark by this time, and we used flashlights to see the

rocks and potholes. The smell of smoke was beginning to be oppressive.

"Must be that grass fire south of town," Mark commented, sniffing.

"Yeah, the wind has really played hell with getting it under control," said Judy. "And now it's heading for the State Forest, with a nice stiff wind to help it along." She shook her head. "After a summer like this one, that's going to be like trying to put out a fire in a box of matches."

"The radio said they brought in some state forestry crews from out of town," said Mark. "I think it's going to be a big one."

We walked another quarter of a mile or so without finding any houses. "When you positively identify the house," Judy told Mark, "I want you to go back to the car and wait for us." She handed him a spare key and he pocketed it.

"You're the deputy," he said.

The houses started up—far apart from one another on parcels of a couple of acres or more. We passed three or four as we walked along, Judy in front with her police flashlight aimed at the ground, me bringing up the rear with a mini-light and Mark in the middle. "That's the place," he said finally, pointing out a smallish frame house set back off the road.

The house had once been white, I assumed, but years of neglect had weathered it to a dirty gray. A wire dog kennel housing two bony pit bulls was visible on one side, and several derelict car bodies were scattered about the yard, held up from the ground by cinder blocks. A dim yellow bulb burned over the front door, casting sickly shadows a distance of a few feet at most. A broken screen door hung off its hinges, creaking in the evening breeze. Heavy curtains covered the windows in the front of the house.

"You're sure?" Judy asked.

"I'm sure," said Mark. "That's the place."

"We'll take it from here, Mark." She shook his hand. "Thanks. We'll be back at the car in about half an hour."

"I don't feel right about leaving you guys," he said. "I know what kind of creeps hang around here."

"I don't think there's going to be any trouble," said Judy, "but I can't take the chance of endangering a minor. Wait for us in the car and we'll be back as soon as we've had a look around."

I gave Mark my flashlight and he headed back the way we had come, but reluctantly. Judy switched off her flashlight and hung it on her belt as we continued on toward the house.

Several cars were already pulled up in the front yard, among them a car Judy recognized as Craig Bellenger's. The rest were unknown. Judy squatted down to see if she could get a look at the license plate numbers, but the available light was against us, and using the flashlight seemed unwise under the circumstances.

In a far corner of the yard I saw a familiar car—a blue sedan like the one that had been keeping me company the last few days. It seemed the reason we hadn't been followed was because the hatchet-faced man was already here. I pointed to the car and made a questioning gesture. Judy shook her head. The car wasn't familiar to her.

We stopped before we got very close to the house and Judy turned her face to the breeze. "The wind's coming from the west," she said in a low whisper. "We'll need to circle around to the east side of the house to stay downwind of the dogs, and keep our distance. We'll approach from the rear. Maybe there's a way to see inside back there."

She led us on a roundabout route through a thickly wooded area to the east that eventually brought us up behind the house. She had shut off her flashlight, and it was slow going through trees and brush with no moon to show the way.

The dogs barked, and someone in the house yelled "Shut up!" They shut up, except for a continuous low growling. We made our way as silently as possible, which was painfully slow. Finally, we arrived at the back of the house.

Bright light poured from a high kitchen window onto the dark ground. We looked up, but despite the fact that no curtain covered the window, it was obvious that there was no way to see inside; the house was built on a hillside, and although the windows in front were at ground level, this opening was several feet over our heads and there was nothing to stand on.

Judy pointed to the window. It was open. I nodded, and we took up positions on opposite sides of the window, listening to the voices coming from the inside.

"You said we were in the clear, that's all I know!" a man's voice said.

"We are in the clear. All you have to do is keep your fucking mouth shut."

"That's Craig!" Judy mouthed at me.

"I *been* keeping my fucking mouth shut," the first man whined. "But what about that detective bitch? She's got my name! She's got your name, too—and Johnny's, and Lauderdale's!"

"She doesn't know anything, Dale," said Craig. "It's all mind games. She's trying to freak us."

"Well, she's freaking me—I was driving the fucking car!"

"I never told you to kill her, asshole," said a third voice, deep and menacing.

"You told me to stop her, Captain. You told me to shut her up," Dale whined.

"You had it right the first time, Dale. You were driving the fucking car." The voice was ripe with menace, and I wondered if Dale was sharp enough to pick up on it. This "Captain" guy would throw Dale to the wolves if any heat came down.

My heart was thumping hard. I'd come to believe Peter and Nora's suspicion that someone in the A.R.C. had been responsible for Cass's death, but overhearing something this close to a confession was not something I'd anticipated. I looked over at Judy. She nodded.

The dogs resumed barking. "Shut those goddamned mutts up!" someone said, and someone else yelled at them again. They whined and quieted down.

"We have to put the heat back on, is all," a fourth voice put in.

"Johnny Hughson," whispered Judy.

"Yeah, well, the last time we put the heat on somebody, they ended up dead." said another voice neither of us recognized.

"It wasn't my fault!" Dale shouted. "I wasn't trying to kill her. The Captain said stop her, and that's all I meant to do, I swear! Scare her bad enough to make her stop."

This was what I'd been waiting for. The exact words. Cass's death had been a homicide and these slimeballs had been scrambling to keep it under wraps. Dale Reid had been driving, but the Captain had given the order, and it was his name I really wanted, or a look at his face.

"I don't think this one scares that easily," said Craig. He was evidently remembering our encounter the previous afternoon. "Nora Lowry's the one who brought her here; we'll just have to convince her it wasn't a very good idea. And if that doesn't work, I'll be glad to teach our little detective a lesson myself."

Craig Bellenger's promise of individual attention did not hearten me. I looked at Judy and got the impression she knew what he might be capable of in that regard. A chill ran over me, not entirely due to the wind. I could taste smoke and ash on my tongue.

"We're not going to mess with Nora Lowry or her kids," a high-pitched voice said. This was definitely Bert Trout. "Eddie would feed us our lungs if we did."

"Eddie'd feed us something else if he knew what really happened to his mother-in-law," Johnny Hughson quipped. "I wonder what he'd think about that."

"If Eddie could think, he wouldn't have shot his mouth off in front of the Lowry bitch in the first place," said Craig. "He knew that only guys from outside are allowed to talk to anyone. I think Eddie's lost his right to tell us who we can and can't deal with. If we put a scare into those kids, Nora'll send that prying pal of hers back up north in a New York minute."

"I'm not doing it. I'm telling you, I'm not going to be the one this time!" Dale was getting closer and closer to hysteria.

"Shut up!" said the Captain. "I'll take care of it, and this time nobody'll get killed. Unless there's no other way. You assholes have to remember that the cause is more important than a life."

I tried to place the Captain's voice, but who could tell anymore? I'd listened to dozens of men's voices trying to find the one on the videotape, and all I got was confusion. The low, menacing snarl that the Captain used in speaking to his subordinates was probably not his normal voice anyway.

My hopes of identifying the talkative man on the tape were also dashed. Evidently they brought in people from other areas to give the speeches, and locals guys were under orders to keep quiet. Leave it to Eddie to defy orders; he was probably very good at that.

The wind shifted. The dogs started up again, in earnest this time, barking and snapping and throwing themselves at the wire mesh of their kennel. Craig said, "Kenny, go check around the house and see what those sons of bitches are going on about."

Judy grabbed my hand and we retraced our earlier route back toward the road. Branches we couldn't see whipped our faces, and every step into the blackness felt like walking over the edge of a pit. I had to fight my natural fear of falling every time I put one foot in front of another, and it took all the self-control I possessed to keep from crying out with each step.

At the front of the house, the dim yellow light illuminated a rusting car hulk. We scrambled over to the car and crouched behind it as the one called Kenny came out the front door. He held a flashlight in one hand and aimed it at various spots around the yard. The beam illuminated the car we were using as cover, then skittered over our heads and lit up the car behind us.

"There's nobody out here," Kenny called back over his shoulder and headed for the kennel.

Judy motioned toward the road and started walking, still crouched down. I followed, but the light grew dimmer the farther we got from the tiny light bulb over the porch, and the car bodies blocked most of that.

We were almost to the road when I stumbled on a rock at the edge of the yard and went down hard. I bit my lip to keep from crying out at the sharp pain in my knee. The dogs started going nuts, hurling themselves at the wire mesh of the kennel.

"What is it, pups?" a young man's voice asked. "What's out there?" He shone the flashlight in our direction and we flattened ourselves to the ground, eating a little dirt in the process. The flashlight beam swept wide circles of light between the kennel and the road, then switched off. "You dummies go back to sleep," said the voice. A moment later the door closed again.

I picked myself up cautiously and helped Judy to her feet. I wiped my mouth with my sleeve as I limped up the road, but nothing could get the grit out of my teeth. We were silent all the way back to the car.

"Jesus, what happened to you guys!" Mark exclaimed when Judy opened the door and the dome light came on.

"Oh, nothing much," said Judy with a smile. She got in and started the car.

"Just a walk in the country," I told him through gritted teeth. There was a scrape on my face and some missing skin on the palms of my hands. Blood ran down my left leg, making a blackish stain on my torn jeans. I didn't want to see what was underneath if it was going to look as awful as it felt.

Mark climbed into the back and I collapsed into the passenger seat. "Thanks, Mark," I said. "We wouldn't even have known about this place without your help."

"So you've got something on these guys now?" he asked.

"We've got something, all right," I replied. "Now we have to figure out what to do with it. And we have to warn Nora."

CHAPTER 25

"I DON'T UNDERSTAND," PETER SAID. "WHY DIDN'T YOU TELL me you were going out there? I would have gone with you." Judy had dropped me off at my car and gone to take Mark home. I'd driven home cautiously, and caused quite a stir as I walked in the front door, striped with dirt and dripping blood onto the entryway tiles.

"I know that, Peter," I said. Nora handed me a damp washcloth and I wiped the top layers of dirt off my face. "I tried to call you this afternoon. Did you get my messages?"

"Yes." He and Nora looked at one another. "We know about Tom. I'm glad you found out about him before we spilled any more valuable information."

"Well, tonight I gave him some information for free, and it got right to the people I wanted it to. They're running scared. I'm sorry I didn't take you along, but I overheard some incriminating conversation, and no harm done."

"Well, almost no harm," said Nora. She pointed to the blood that was seeping through my pants leg.

"Okay, I scraped my knee."

"And your face, and your hands . . ."

"It didn't seem like a good idea to turn on the flashlight," I said, pulling the bloody fabric away from my knee and wincing at the unpleasant sensation. "I think I'm going to take a shower, and then I'll let you bandage this mess. We have a lot to talk about when I get down. Is there any white rum in the house?"

"I'll have a drink waiting when you get downstairs," said Peter. He followed me out of the kitchen and put a hand on my arm as I started up the stairs. "Caley, did they kill her?"

I covered his hand with mine and swallowed the lump in my throat. "Yes. I think they did."

"I think Nora should take the boys and get out of town right away." Peter leaned forward in his chair and took Nora's hands to stop them from shaking. The living room was lit by one tiny copper mesh lamp on the mantel, which cast a deep golden light into the dimness.

Nora nodded at Peter. "Yes, I've got to get out of this place. I've got to get Matt and Harry away from here. Tomorrow you guys can drive us to Sacramento and we'll get a hotel room or something."

"I've got a better idea," said Peter. "I'm going to make a phone call." He let go of Nora's hand and walked into the kitchen. I drank my second drink and waited for my stomach to unclench.

"Eddie's one of them," Nora said dully. "You're sure?"

"I'm sure. Apparently the reason they never threatened you or your kids was because they were afraid of what he'd do to them."

"And you don't think he was one of the ones who . . ."

"He doesn't know. But he's part of it, Nora. He's one of them. And even if he's tried to protect you so far, he might not be able to protect you now. Peter's right. You need to leave tonight."

Peter came out of the kitchen. "Danny's car is back from the shop. He'll be here in a few minutes to drive you to my house in San Francisco. He'll stay there with you until this is over," he told her.

"It's over now," Nora said, looking back and forth between Peter and me. "None of us can stay here. If I go, they'll just hurt one of you. Maybe they didn't set out to kill Mom, but she's dead. You can't let them kill you, too!"

"It's not over, Nora," said Peter. "They're still out there." He turned to me. "Caley, I think you should quit the case. They've targeted you, too."

"Only because I'm handy and visible. They're going to go after whoever gets in their way, you know that."

"That's why you should leave. You've put yourself in danger, and it's time to get out while you can."

"He's right, Caley," said Nora. "You've done all you can."

There it was—my out if I wanted it. I could leave now and everyone would pat me on the back and say "You've done all you can." But would they really believe it?

Would I?

"I'm staying," I told them. "We haven't beaten those bastards yet."

Peter nodded, acknowledging my right to choose foolhardiness over security. "You'd better start packing," he told Nora.

Nora got up from her chair and sighed. "I feel like a coward, but I can't stay. The boys need me."

"They've been through enough," I told her. "They can't stay here any longer, and neither can you."

Nora went upstairs to pack and wake Matt and Harry. Peter sat on the couch beside me. "I'm scared out of my wits," he confessed. "How about you?"

Fear had already made a little nest in my stomach and was settling in for a long stay. I let out a deep breath I didn't know I was holding, and nodded.

"What now?" he asked.

"We stake out the house," I said. "We watch who comes and goes and then we watch them, too. We find out who gave Dale the order."

I finished my drink and Peter got up to pour me another, which I accepted gratefully. I felt too tired to move a muscle, and my eyelids weighed a pound apiece, but I wasn't sure I'd be able to sleep tonight with this fluttering lump in my stomach and my brain on fire.

"I don't know if any higher-ups in the Sheriff's Department are involved," I said to Peter. "Bellenger never mentioned anything specific to Judy, but how much stock can we put in that?"

"Will Judy help us on this?"

"I think so. Judy's a good resource. She hates those guys." I closed my eyes. Peter put a woolen lap robe over me and for a few minutes I hovered between consciousness and an anxious doze. Danny's knock brought me out of it instantly. I spilled rum on my bathrobe as I jumped several inches, then settled down to shaking with relief.

Peter took the glass out of my hand and set it down on the side table, then went to let Danny in.

Danny sat down across from Peter and me and looked back and forth between us. "Are we all leaving?" he asked.

Peter and I looked at one another. "No," I answered for both of us. "Not all of us."

"From what you told me on the phone," Danny said, "they ran Cass off the road. Are you going to hang around until they kill you, too? How do you plan to defend yourselves from them? Caley, do you own a gun?"

"Yes, I do." I didn't mention that I hadn't carried it in over a month and couldn't bring myself even to pick it up.

"Well, Peter doesn't," said Danny, pointing at his friend. "He refuses to own one, or any other kind of weapon, and if you gave him one he wouldn't use it, even to save his own life. Am I right, Peter?"

Peter looked down at the floor. "I can't use violence against another human being, Danny. You know that as well as anyone."

"Not even to save your life."

Peter shook his head.

"How about to save someone else's life?"

Peter looked up slowly, first at Danny, then at me. "I don't know," he said, so quietly I could barely hear him.

"You know I respect your decision to be nonviolent," Danny said. "And I understand it. But you're in a whole new game here. These people don't have your principles. They don't have any principles I recognize. I want you to think about protecting yourself."

"The plan is to get enough evidence to get the case reopened," Peter said. "If we're careful, we can do that without attracting too much more attention to ourselves."

"Since when were you careful?" Danny asked Peter. "When you were illegally entering a nuclear test site and getting yourself and a hundred other people hauled into jail? When you were leading antiwar protests at the Federal Building in San Francisco and debating politics with belligerent pro-war goons? When you were getting lumps raised on your head by Chicago policemen?"

He stood up and ran a hand through his hair, looking down at Peter. "You don't know the meaning of the word 'careful' when you're out to prove something."

"Danny, you always worried too much about me," Peter said. "You and Elias both."

Danny blinked back tears. "I just wonder how many more friends I have to lose," he said in a whisper.

Nora came to the bottom of the stairs, a sleepy twin under each arm. Danny picked up Harry and carried him out the front door to his car. Peter took Matt and followed him. Nora and I went upstairs for the luggage.

"It's not too late to change your mind," she told me, handing me a suitcase. "We could all go to San Francisco together, and I could buy you a ticket back up to Cascade. Think about it."

I shook my head. "I *have* thought about it. It's tempting, but not tempting enough."

Nora moved to the door, then turned and looked around her room as though memorizing it. "I don't think I'll be back," she said.

I left her in the doorway and started down the stairs with a suitcase, legs trembling just a little.

I was as sure I had to stay as I'd been a few minutes ago, but a lot more frightened now that I knew Peter was a pacifist. I hadn't thought I was counting on him to come to my rescue—I've learned to do that for myself over the years—but to know that he was steadfastly against using violence for any reason seemed to remove a support I hadn't even known I was leaning on. Peter might stop a bullet for me, or for anyone, but he wouldn't fire one. Would I?

Last time my life was saved, it was a bullet that did the job. That time, I'd been able to fire it myself. Could I do it again? The sight of my trusty Walther made me sick to my stomach.

The thought of pointing it at a human being again made my insides turn to ice.

I put the last of Nora's luggage into the back of Danny's car, and Peter and I stood on the porch and watched them drive away. I wondered if he was thinking the same thing I was: that if we had more brains and less stubborn determination, we'd be right behind them.

"I think I owe you an explanation," said Peter after Danny's taillights had winked out behind the oak trees lining the road.

"No, you don't," I told him. "You don't have to explain why you don't want to kill anyone. I don't want to kill anyone, either." I turned and went back inside.

Peter followed me, closing the door. "I made a decision a long time ago about this," he said. "It was a necessary one for me." He held up the bottle of rum and I nodded wearily. I'd feel like total shit in the morning, but maybe I could get the kinks out of my stomach tonight. I turned on another lamp and sat down on one of the couches.

"Inside, I'm as violent a person as anyone I've ever known," Peter said, handing me a glass of rum with ice cubes. "There are some men out there who might want to hurt us, even kill us, I don't know. They killed Cass, and no part of me wants to forgive any of them for that."

He poured a drink for himself and sat down on the couch opposite me. "What I really want, deep inside where I don't look very often, is to kill every one of them."

Peter stared up at the high ceiling, a deep weariness in his weathered face. "Something happened in my life, Caley, a long time ago. I hurt someone who was beating up on a friend of mine. This was during an antiwar demonstration maybe twenty-five years ago, and the cops got nervous and started laying into us. My friend went down under this one cop's stick, and he was just lying there and the cop was still beating on him and I got mad. I took the stick away from the cop, and when he went for his gun I broke his hand. Then I hit him some more.

"I told myself I was doing it to help my friend, but what I couldn't avoid recognizing even at the time was that I was enjoying it. I felt like I had a *right* to do it. Like I was right and that made anything I did right, too.

"I hurt this man badly, sent him to the hospital. For a day and a half they thought he was going to die, and it changed my whole life and everything in it. If I hadn't made a solemn promise on everything I loved to turn my life completely around, I think someday I might have killed someone. If I took up a gun now, feeling the way I do now, I *know* I would. I don't think I could survive that."

I knocked back half the drink and shuddered at the bite of the rum against my throat. "I'm one up on you, Peter," I told him, holding my glass up to the light. "I *have* killed someone, and I *did* survive it. What I don't know, what I can't even begin to guess, is whether I'd be able to do it again."

It was almost funny if you looked at it right. Here I'd been going around for the past month or so imagining Death dogging my heels, and trying to get as far from it as I could. Now there was a very real possibility, regardless of what we had told Nora and Danny, that we were putting ourselves in Death's way, and instead of running away, we were flagging the sonofabitch down. I managed a tired laugh, and Peter looked at me curiously.

"What are we getting ourselves into, here?" he wondered.

"Trouble," I said. "A whole world of trouble."

CHAPTER 26

IT WAS ALMOST LIGHT WHEN I FINALLY CLIMBED THE STAIRS to the guest room. Four drinks, about twice as many as I allow myself even on special occasions, lulled me into an uneasy sleep troubled by dreams of hooded men and fire. When I woke up I smelled the reason—the smoke in the air was thick enough to burn my eyes. Evidently the fire had not been contained during the night, but had gotten far worse. The shriek of fire alarms that had brought me out of sleep was the ringing of a telephone, and Mickey's hands pointed to seven o'clock.

I stumbled into the hall and picked up the phone. "Caley, this is Judy. I had a phone call from Craig this morning."

"Sweet Jesus," I groaned. "How bad was it?"

"You were right," she said. "He figured me for ratting on him, and he was pretty graphic about what he has in mind as a payback."

"You'd better blow town for a while, girl."

"I'm way ahead of you. I'm an hour out of town in my own car and no tail."

"Don't tell me any more."

"I won't. I'm calling in sick—I've got a few days' sick leave saved up. How's everything there?"

"Nora and the boys are out of town. They're safe."

"You're not."

"I can't leave just yet. With any luck, though, I'll be on my way home tomorrow."

"That's plenty of time for them to get to you," she said.

"Peter and I are sticking together until this is over. No one's going to find me alone."

"You own a gun?"

How many people now had prescribed a gun for my problems? I'd lost count. I wondered how many of them were as intimately acquainted with what guns do as I was. "Yeah," I replied wearily. "I own a gun."

"Keep it loaded and keep it handy," Judy advised. "I'm going to get hold of a friend who retired from the Department last year. He's cool, and he should be able to tell me who we can trust inside. Then we'll have someplace to go with what we've found out. Keep your head down and I'll call you back tonight."

I thought about keeping my head down. It was a safe position, but not one from which I could gather much information. I also thought about going back to bed, but sleep would be an impossibility now that I had given thought to my current situation.

Sighing, I plodded downstairs and rummaged through the cupboards. Still no coffee. I boiled water for tea and drank two cups before Peter joined me. We sat and watched the smoky light through the high kitchen windows, each lost in our own thoughts—our own doubts.

"We have to call Dolores," Peter said finally. "We need to let her know what you found out."

"I think we ought to let Tim Wynand know, too," I said. "He's been helpful to us, and he cares about what we're doing."

Peter seemed to think about this for a few moments. "Okay," he said finally. "I'll call him."

I went upstairs to shower myself into some semblance of humanity while Peter made the phone calls. On the way, I noticed a slip of paper beside the living room phone that had been there since sometime yesterday. "While You Were Out," it said in black print, and below that in someone's handwriting: "David Hayden called." I clutched it in my hand on the way upstairs as though it might have some comfort for me.

I stood by the upstairs hall phone for half a minute, but I didn't want to call David for fear I'd blurt out what was going on in my life right now. I was afraid his concern for my safety would bring me to my senses—and that was the last thing I needed. I showered, put a fresh bandage on my knee, and got dressed. On my way out I put the message in the pocket of my jeans.

Dolores and Tim were both in town on Saturdays, so Cedar Ridge seemed like the best place for all of us to get together. Our usual meeting spot having been ruled out for obvious reasons, we decided to meet at Chiang's Garden. Even given that it was hard to know who to trust anymore, Patty and Martin Chiang seemed a safe bet not to be gathering information for the American Rescue Coalition, and they were open for breakfast.

We were all together in Chiang's private dining room in back by nine o'clock. The front part of the restaurant was nearly deserted, but we didn't need the added complication of having to stop talking every time a local customer walked by the table.

Dolores moved a chair out of her way and rolled up to the table, the last to arrive. Patty Chiang had brought a thermal carafe and four brown china mugs, and was pouring coffee all around. "Are you ready to eat now?" she asked with a friendly smile. She memorized each person's order as she had two nights before at dinner. I still couldn't figure that one out—I was obviously not cut out for restaurant work.

I looked from face to face as Patty went around the table taking orders for breakfast. All these people had loved Cass and lost her forever. I had already caused Peter, Nora, and Danny even more distress by confirming their suspicions that her death had not been accidental but a deliberate act on the part of someone else—someone who reacted with fear and hatred to her opposition of their political views. Now it was my task to do the same favor for Dolores and Tim. Would this information lessen their pain? I couldn't imagine it would.

Everyone wants the truth, and everyone suffers for it because it's so seldom what we want to hear. I took this case because I wanted to help the people who loved Cass, but also because I have this unquenchable thirst for the truth, even though when I find it I sometimes want to give it back. I stayed with it because there are people who preach hate and hide their faces and rule by fear, and I don't believe those kinds of people should be allowed to take over our lives.

Frank Dietrich said you change things one person at a time. One person is all any of us can offer up for change, and I was offering my own actions, for what they were worth. I just hoped I could do it without causing any further harm to Cass Lowry's friends and family.

Peter was holding up well, considering he already knew what I had to say. Some of the grief in his eyes had been replaced by resolution. I knew he wouldn't rest until we'd gotten to the bottom of this. And at the bottom was something horrible.

Dolores was still playing "tough old bird," but I could tell it was wearing on her. Too much death and treachery had visited in too short a time. Her eyes seemed years older than when I had first seen her the day of the funeral.

Tim seemed focused inward somewhere, trying hard to control some inner demon. I had succeeded in making him believe that Cass was murdered. Did he need that burden on top of the fact that he'd never stopped loving her?

"Danny and Nora aren't here because they're hiding out from the American Rescue Coalition," I began.

"Dear God, what happened?" Dolores asked, her face ashen.

I reached out and touched her hand. "Nothing happened. We got Nora out of town because I overheard someone talking about threatening her kids. Danny went with her, to make sure she stays safe."

"But I thought . . ."

"Apparently the A.R.C. boys are in this too deep to let fear of Eddie Shepard slow them down. They want to get rid of me by scaring Nora, so we put Nora out of their reach."

"So now they can go directly for you," Tim said, an edge of anger showing through his concern.

"I never said it was a perfect plan," I replied.

I gave Dolores and Tim a rundown of my activities of the previous night, and the implications of the conversation Judy Roy and I had overheard. Tim sat with his fists clenched against his lips the whole time, occasionally shaking his head. Dolores interrupted periodically with an exclamation of surprise. Peter had heard it before, but that probably didn't do much to blunt the pain.

"Sounds like they're pretty eager to get you off this case," said Dolores when I stopped talking. "Do you think it's safe for you to stick around?"

I glanced over at Peter, my moral support in foolhardiness. "Safe enough," I said, not sure whether or not that could be called an outright lie. "When we ID the Captain, I'll be happy to step aside and let the sheriffs handle this. Of course we don't know yet how many of them are involved, either. I have someone checking that out for me."

"Caley and I think this would be exactly the wrong time to back down," said Peter. "The fact they're this scared means we've got them on the ropes. We just sent Nora and the boys away so they could feel safer."

"Wouldn't it have been simpler just to drop the case?" asked Tim. "If they're that determined to get rid of you, they might not stop at threats."

"If we drop the case now," said Peter, "the man responsible for Cass's death may go free. Caley could testify that someone named Dale admitted he was driving a car and tried to frighten someone and they died, but that's not enough even to convict Dale Reid of manslaughter. It's going to take identifying the person really responsible."

"All I want is the name or the face of the man who gave the order," I told Tim. "I want the 'Captain.' Once I identify him, I'll be happy to see the last of Cedar Ridge."

The air outside the restaurant was thick with smoke, and traffic was almost entirely absent since the roads to the south of town had been closed to all but firefighting vehicles. Dolores drove off for her store, and Tim stayed in front of Chiang's with us for a few moments, looking troubled.

"We're going to be careful, Tim," I told him. "We'll have more information soon, and we'll know who it's safe to take it to. This is almost over."

"I wonder," he said, looking across the highway at the trees and houses of Cedar Ridge. "I wonder if it *is* over. All of it."

A few tourists wandered through the streets, unwilling to allow their vacations to be dictated by the whims of nature or random arsonists, whichever was responsible, but the constant influx of cars from the north had slowed to a trickle as word of the fire's spread made the news. It had invaded the nearby forest and was spreading through the dry pines and firs at an alarming rate. The annual fireworks display, scheduled for this evening, had been canceled. The sickly color of the sunlight had intensified, painting the world a repulsive shade of yellow-brown-gray. A few flags atop poles in front of nearby stores hung listlessly in the heat.

Peter and I had decided not to let one another out of sight from now on when we were away from the house. When it got dark again we planned to make another visit to the meeting house. If no one was there, we'd let ourselves in and have a look around.

With so much police protection going for them, the Men's Club might not have been too careful about what kind of identifying evidence they left around. The more names and faces we had, the surer we were to get to the Captain eventually. I noted that I hadn't seen my shadow in the blue sedan so far today. Well, the day was young.

Our next stop was the bookstore to tell the morning clerk that Nora wouldn't be in. Several customers were already in the store, including Maureen Adler and Mike McCutcheon. Mike was lost in an old car restorer's catalog, his back to the door, and didn't see us come in. Maureen looked up from a home decorating magazine and gave us a poisonously sweet smile.

Peter and the clerk went over the store schedule at the front counter, trying to put together a strategy for running the store without Nora. I tiptoed toward the science fiction aisle, hoping Mike wouldn't notice I was there.

In the science fiction section I found a Connie Willis book to replace the one Jake had borrowed and couldn't bring himself to return, and browsed a bit among the new releases. When I heard the cash register beeping, I peeked over the top of the rack. Mike paid for his catalog and left the store.

"You and Peter spending a lot of time together these days?" Maureen inquired behind me.

I engraved a pleasant expression on my face and turned around. "He's my client," I said. "I report my findings to him." As interested as Maureen was in other people's affairs, she could scarcely have missed learning the real reason I was in town, so there didn't seem to be any point in continuing the "visiting family friend" charade.

"I certainly hope you're not going to cause any more bad publicity for Cedar Ridge," Maureen said, her expression darkening. "This town got along just fine without people coming in here causing unpleasantness and stirring things up."

I spent half a second wondering if there was still any reason to be remotely pleasant to Maureen. There wasn't one, at least one that I could find in that length of time. "I've noticed that when you stir this town up very hard," I said, "horrible things dart out of dark corners. Now, why don't you scurry off and sell a house or something?"

I turned around and walked off in the other direction, but not before I got a glimpse of Maureen Adler's mouth hanging open, framed by sugar-pink lips. I took a circuitous route to the cash register. Maureen took the fastest way to the door, and slammed it on her way out.

"What do you suppose got into her?" the clerk inquired.

"Darned if I know," I replied innocently, and paid for my book.

I felt like we ought to visit the Coffee Pot, so as not to alert Tom Flanders that anything might be wrong, but I was genuinely worried about Peter's ability to act nonchalant under the circumstances. "I'm not sure you're going to be able to pretend you don't want to rip his head off and spit down his neck," I told him. "It's not that easy for me, even. Why don't you drop me off? I'll meet you at the Forty-Niner after I've chatted him up a bit."

"We agreed we'd go everywhere together except the bathroom," Peter said, frowning over at me from behind the steering wheel.

"We can skip it, then," I said, hoping he'd take me up on the offer. "It's not really that important if we don't go in there every single day."

"No, you were right the first time. Let's go have an iced tea," Peter said, getting into the turn lane as the Coffee Pot came up on our left. His eyes were rock-hard, almost frightening above his smile. "Let's make sure old Tom feels all those friendly vibrations."

Tom was there to greet us at the door, and he was so anxious to please that he didn't seem capable of noticing any subtle changes in Peter's attitude. A few minutes spent sipping tea in the back room with Tom pulled up to our table assured us that he was still our good buddy.

We discussed the case with him without telling him anything new, but being very free with the old information. He seemed genuinely pleased to hear all of it. "Those drinks are on the house," he assured us as we got up to go. "I didn't even write up a ticket for them."

Kay Flanders searched my eyes for some sort of reassurance as I walked past her. I didn't have it to give. It might be her job to protect Tom from his own stupidity, but it sure as hell wasn't mine.

Peter's performance was better than I could have expected, and it wasn't until we were back in the parking lot and walking away from the restaurant that he allowed the rage he was feeling inside to emerge. His eyes seemed almost to film over with anger, so that I took his arm for fear he couldn't see to walk.

"You'll never have to do that again," I assured him. "We'll be through with this before you ever have to lay eyes on Tom Flanders again this side of a courtroom."

Peter let out a deep, ragged breath. "I think I need a drink," he said.

"I know just the place," I told him.

CHAPTER 27

OUR REAL WORK WOULDN'T BEGIN UNTIL NEARLY DARK, AND it was not quite noon now, so we killed an hour and a half at the Forty-Niner talking to Frank Dietrich and sipping ice cold Watneys. Frank and Peter weren't acquainted, since Peter didn't frequent the local bars, but they took to one another instantly, as I'd suspected they would.

Having a kindred spirit to talk to seemed to take a weight off Peter's shoulders. Frank's "small-town boy learns about the wide world" stories, dispensed between waiting on customers as the saloon began to fill up with bored tourists, made us laugh in spite of ourselves, and that kept the worst of our fears at bay for a while.

Lunchtime came and went, but neither of us were hungry. We switched to coffee and took a table where we could talk over our plans, such as they were, for tonight.

"There are two possible ways to go about this that I can see," I told Peter. "We can put ourselves out in the open and keep asking questions around town like I've been doing the past three days. The upside is, it might make the bad guys even more nervous."

"And the downside?"

"It might make them *too* nervous. What I really need to know is the identity of the Captain. The way the jungle telegraph works in this town, I'm likely to spook him right into hiding."

I drained my coffee. Frank brought over a fresh pot and filled it. I made a connection in my mind and looked around the room for locals before I said anything about it—a habit I'd gotten into lately. "There's this man who was following me around for a few days," I said to Peter and Frank. "He's dark with very sharp, strong features and pale eyes. Thin, and probably tall, though I've never seen him standing. Does that sound familiar to either of you?"

Peter shook his head. "Not anyone I know," he said.

"Doesn't sound like anyone I've seen in here," said Frank. "And I don't get out all that often." He took the pot back behind the bar.

"This guy's car was at the meeting house last night," I told Peter. "Judy and I ID'd most of the voices we heard, but there were a couple we didn't know. I'm wondering if he could be our 'Captain.' He wouldn't have to be from around here, after all. The A.R.C. has tentacles all over the state—all over the country, for that matter. They're pretty well established in the local Sheriff's Department, and I'm thinking this guy could be law enforcement, too."

Peter nodded. "Hence the 'Captain' part. It's a possibility. So what's the other tactic you had in mind?" he asked.

"Lay low until it's almost time to go out to the meeting house. They may wonder what we're up to—with any luck they might even think we're backing off. Then we could take a big stick and stir up the hornets' nest a little."

"What stick did you have in mind?"

"Eddie Shepard. He's always had a short fuse, and I think I know just how to light it."

I called the fire station, and the man on the phone informed me that Eddie was on the fire line, but would be back for a couple of hours this evening before he had to go out again. He should be there by six, the man told me, and did I want to leave my name. "I think I'll just surprise him," I said.

At six, we were at the fire station. Eddie was there, just

back from the fire zone. Soot blackened him everywhere his clothes didn't cover, and his clothes were as black as his face. He had thrown off his fire suit and was plunging his arms into a sinkful of soapy water when we came up behind him.

He turned around and sighed heavily when he saw me. "What the fuck do you want now, Caley?" he asked with no pretense at patience or politeness. He ignored Peter entirely.

"I know you're not having a terrific day," I began.

"You're goddamned right I'm not," he almost shouted. His voice rang in the nearly empty building. "I've been on the fire lines fourteen goddamned hours, and after I cop maybe two hours sleep and meet up with some volunteers from the State Department of Forestry, I'll be back out there all night."

He grabbed a bristle brush and scrubbed at his arms and hands. "We've already lost two guys to heatstroke. One of them may be permanently fried. When your brain gets too hot, sometimes it just goes south, you know? And sometimes it never comes back. And this motherfucker of a fire just keeps getting bigger and eating trees."

"Like I said, I'm really sorry to bother you right now, but I have some information you may find interesting."

"Such as what?" He didn't sound too interested.

"Dale Reid was driving the car that ran Cass off the road. Someone called 'the Captain' gave the order. They want me off the case bad enough to try to get to Nora through your sons."

Now I had his attention. He turned from the sink, arms dripping black soapy water onto the floor. "Nobody would dare touch Nora or my boys," he said.

"Craig Bellenger seems to think different. And so does the Captain."

"I'll kill the motherfuckers," he growled. I believed him.

Peter handed him a towel that had been hanging on a hook over the sink, and Eddie dried his arms and scrubbed at his face with the damp cloth. It came away black.

"Who's the Captain, Eddie?" I asked him. "What's his name?"

Eddie glared at me and pushed past me into an adjoining

room. I tried to follow, but another firefighter barred my way. "You can't go back there, ma'am," he said. "Those are the barracks rooms."

I hurried outside and Peter followed. We circled the building, looking for another way in. We stopped at every window and peered inside hoping for a glimpse of Eddie. Finally, we got one.

He was holding a phone receiver in front of his face, his knuckles pale under a film of soot. "Be there!" he screamed into the receiver. "You be there or I'll come and find you wherever you are!" He threw the phone against the wall and grabbed a shirt from a locker near a bed.

Peter and I bolted for the front of the building. We met Eddie coming out of the big garage door.

He paused a moment at the door to the office. "You tell Williamson he's got my crew," he told the man inside. "I'm out of here."

"Wait!" the man shouted. He got up from his seat and chased Eddie to his car. "You can't just take off like that!"

Eddie walked around him and got into the car. "Watch me," he said as he slammed the door. The man turned and walked back to the office, shaking his head in disgust.

I reached the driver's door just as Eddie started the engine. I grabbed the door as he slammed the gearshift into reverse. "Nora took the boys and went out of town," I said breathlessly. "They're safe."

"You don't know these assholes like I do," he snarled. "I'm not ever going to feel safe about letting them near my family." He stomped on the gas, tearing my hands off the door and spraying gravel in a rooster tail as he spun the car around, then shooting up more rocks and dirt as he went into first gear and gunned out of the driveway. He was down the road and out of sight before the dust settled.

Peter came up to stand beside me. "Where do you think he's going?"

I thought back to Eddie's phone conversation of a minute before. "Be there!" he had told the person at the other end. Be where? "I think I know where," I told him. We got back into my car and drove in the direction Eddie had gone.

It wasn't as easy to find the meeting house again as I'd thought it would be. I repeated the turns of the night before as best I could remember them, but my sense of direction was thoroughly confused by the tangle of tree-lined two-lane roads that looked more similar than different. I worried the whole time that someone might come by and recognize me, or that I might pick up my friendly local tail again, but the few cars we saw up close paid no attention to us, and the man in the dark blue sedan was nowhere in sight.

Eventually I recognized the place where Judy had pulled off the road the night before, and knew I could find the house on foot, but it was still too light to approach it very closely. At least we should be able to see if Eddie's car was there and what other cars might be around, I thought.

We continued another half-mile or so up the road until I recognized one of the houses we had passed while walking last night. We found a clump of trees off the side of the road and left the car there, though it was still more conspicuous than I would have liked. I took a couple of dark shirts out of the back seat, and we put them on over our clothes and headed in the general direction of the house, avoiding the road as much as possible.

I pulled a gray scarf out of my shirt pocket and covered my hair, tying it in a knot on the back of my neck. In the sunlight, red hair is like a beacon. When I was a little girl my father used to say I looked like someone had set my head on fire. It was not an image I liked then, and I liked it even less now.

My injured knee began to complain as we tramped over the uneven ground, stepping over rocks and logs and hoping there were no irritable reptiles napping underneath. It was a slower and less panicked trek than the night before, but the closer I got to the place, the more my stomach knotted up. I really should have had something to eat, I thought. Then if I threw up, there'd be some point to it.

Finally I could make out the shape of the house through the trees and bushes. We stopped to take inventory of the yard. Eddie's car was pulled up almost to the front door, and a couple of other cars were there too, besides the full complement of rusted wrecks. One was a station wagon sporting a "Bring Back America" bumper sticker—the other a Camaro with more bondo surface than original metal. It might even have been there last night—I probably would have mistaken it for one of the wrecks.

The pit bulls lay listlessly in the dust, crowded into the one shady spot in their kennel, waiting for the temperature to drop. Their bony sides moved slightly up and down with the rhythm of their breathing. I felt a pang of sympathy for them—even in the shade of the trees the heat was formidable.

I looked around. We were in a pretty good position if we wanted to wait out the rest of the day right here. We were well hidden from the house and the road by trees and scrub, and the nearest other house was several hundred yards away. "Shall we?" I said, indicating a likely spot on the ground.

"Why not?" said Peter. He sat down cross-legged and I sat nearby where I could lean up against a rock. The view through a stand of buck brush was as good as a one-way mirror. From here we could see any comings and goings without fear of giving away our location. To anyone looking this way from the house or yard, we'd be just two dark clumps in the brush.

There was shouting coming from the house, but we couldn't make out any words. I itched to get closer, but I knew once I got on the other side of the brush I'd be highly visible against the dirt and dried grass of the yard. After a few minutes, the shouting stopped. The wind came up, hot and gritty, carrying the scent of ash and wood smoke.

Mickey's hands pointed to six-thirty, then seven. I was aware of thirst. I leaned back against the granite rock, which felt a lot more comfortable than it had a few minutes ago.

"Caley! Wake up!" Peter was shaking my shoulder and speaking in an urgent whisper. I opened my eyes to near-darkness. "Look over there!" Peter was saying.

Someone was coming around the side of the house from the back, dragging a large sack. He pulled on it with both hands, digging his heels into the dry ground, then dropped the end he'd been holding with a grunt audible from our hiding place. The dogs leaped against the sides of their kennel, barking and growling. "Shut up," he told them without conviction.

He stood and looked around the immediate area briefly, then walked around to the back.

"Let's go check it out," I suggested. We got up and dusted off our clothes as though we needed to be presentable, then crept out of our brush hideaway and into the open. No one had turned on the porch light, so it was almost totally dark in the yard. The moon was setting in the west, but even that pale light was clouded by the smoke that choked the sky.

Lights blinded me. I grabbed Peter's arm and dove back into the buck brush as a car turned in from the road. Rocks and branches punished us for our lack of foresight. We lay there perfectly still as the driver pulled into the yard and shut off the engine. The dogs started up again, thundering their indignation at the intruder.

I moved my head slowly in that direction to get a look at the car. It was dark blue, and the man getting out of it was tall and thin, with dark hair. Any more detail was guesswork, but I knew it was him—the man with the knife-edge features and pale gray eyes. He'd taken on mythic proportions in my mind of late, but I wasn't about to get up and ask him for his autograph.

He knocked lightly and walked in the front door, closing it behind him. Before I could get completely to my feet, two more cars pulled up. Tom Flanders pulled his red pickup into a spot on the far side of a rusted-out truck, probably meaning to conceal it from the road. Dale Reid pulled in next to him and followed him into the house. After a minute, the dogs settled down again, whining occasionally.

I got up cautiously and Peter followed. As dark as it was, I could see that his face was scratched from the dive into the brush, and from the stinging I could feel everywhere I wasn't covered by clothing, it was a good bet I didn't look much better.

"We'll go around that side of the house, the same way Judy and I went last night," I told Peter. "If we follow the same route and go slow, we should be safe from tripping. I don't want to use flashlights unless we absolutely have to."

"Lead on," Peter said, gesturing me ahead. "You know the way."

We crouched down and headed across the yard, keeping car bodies between us and the house windows as much as possible. The hot breeze stirred the dead grass as we passed.

Something heavy crashed against a metal mesh fence and howled. The dogs. Shit! I'd forgotten about the wind! The second dog took up the cry, gnashing its teeth on the kennel fence with a sound that would have sent a chill up my spine if I'd been able to spare the time.

We were closer to the house than the stand of buck brush. One meant almost certain safety and the other might mean an end to this case. I made a dash for the side of the house, deep in shadow. The dogs threw themselves against the kennel fence over and over, their barking becoming more and more frantic.

The front door banged open. The relative safety of the shadow was just ahead when something caught my foot and sent me sprawling onto something large and resilient lying on the ground. Peter fell on top of me, then rolled away. Our hands met as we explored the object, wrapped in burlap. I pulled at the fabric, put my hand inside—and touched a human face, slack and a bit cold. I gasped and pulled my hand back.

I could still hear the dogs, as from a great distance, through a ringing in my ears, and I remembered how pretty much this same thing had happened when I was eleven and my appendix ruptured. I was getting ready to pass out.

"There's somebody out here!" a man shouted from the front door. "Turn those dogs loose!"

I heard the clanging of a metal gate, and seconds later the labored breathing of men and dogs galloping closer. Now I *wanted* to pass out, but I couldn't. Out of the darkness, a huge mouth full of teeth lunged at my face and there was the snap of jaws and the snap of a chain pulling tight.

"Well, look here," said a voice on the other end of the chain. "Bubba's found us some burglars." The dog pulled against the restraint, his choke collar digging a furrow in his neck. He roared his rage at me, spraying me with hot splashes of saliva. The second dog was still bellowing at Peter, also held in check by a man and a chain. Peter looked up past my shoulder as someone stepped up behind me, shining a flashlight beam onto my face. I turned to look.

"Welcome to the new America, Miss Burke."

"Fuck you, Bellenger," I replied. Good manners probably wouldn't have done me much good anyway, the way I figured it.

He handed the dog over to the man behind him and knelt down very close to my head. "You may yet get your chance," he whispered into my ear, then lifted me up by my hair and backhanded me across the face. Tears sprang into my eyes as a wave of stinging pain obliterated every other feeling except hate. Bellenger dropped me again and got to his feet.

"Hey, Captain," the second man called. He shone his flashlight on us, and on Eddie Shepard, whose dead body lay underneath us, face free of the burlap wrapping, eyes staring at the scene with nearly as much dismay as I felt right then. "Look who's here to see you!"

A third man walked toward the circle of light, an automatic weapon slung casually in the crook of his arm. "I thought it might be our little detective," he said as he approached.

One of the men directed his flashlight toward him. "We didn't have to go find them, Captain. They walked right up and said hello."

"I was hoping they would," said Mike McCutcheon. "This makes everything a whole lot easier."

CHAPTER 28

. . . .

"I CAN TAKE CARE OF THIS FOR YOU, CAPTAIN," SAID THE hatchet-faced man. He stepped between Bellenger and me and pulled me to my feet. "I'll just take them for a little drive."

"No way!" Bellenger shouted at Mike, pulling on my other arm. "No way Lauderdale gets to do this! You promised me!"

Mike laughed softly. "Devotion to duty is a good thing in a soldier, Bellenger." He kicked the burlap sack. "Eddie could have used a little more devotion to duty."

He waved Lauderdale off. "Craig's been a good boy and he wants his reward," he said, putting a spin of ridicule on the words. "This little lady pissed him off pretty good the other day, and he's got a lousy sense of humor about things like that."

"He's personally involved," Lauderdale insisted. "He'll be careless and leave evidence. Leave this to me, and there won't be any evidence."

"Leave it, Lauderdale," Mike said. "This one's Bellenger's. The faggot-lover, too." He signaled Bert Trout, who motioned Peter to his feet and kept a gun trained on him. "They're both Bellenger's." The dogs looked back and forth between us, snarling, waiting for enough slack to strike.

A young boy about Mark's age came running up, breathless. "We found the car, Captain. It's parked in some trees down the road." He pointed in the direction from which we had come to the house.

"Good job, Kenny," said Mike. "You take Bubba and Queenie back to the kennel, then wait in the house. You go along with him," he said to the men who were holding the dogs. "We'll talk about what to do with Eddie when I join you. Bert, get her car keys and bring back the car."

Bert fumbled in my pockets for my key ring. I couldn't help him, having Bellenger on one arm and Lauderdale on the other, but I probably wouldn't have been all that cooperative, anyway.

"Dale, you're going to be riding with Craig," Mike said.

"I don't want him along," said Bellenger. "I can do this myself."

"Dale's going along to find you a way into the fire zone on the back roads," said Mike. "Lauderdale wants no evidence, we're giving him no evidence."

I think that's when I first realized I was going to die.

Mike continued barking orders. "Bert, you follow to pick Dale and Craig up. You'll be leaving her car there."

"I'd like to go along," said Lauderdale. "I'd like to make sure this is done right."

"You ride with Bert, then. When it's done, everybody go their separate ways and I don't want to say more than hello to you in town for the next two months. We're gonna lay low and start up small after everything cools down. All right? Let's get going, then."

Bert drove my car into the driveway. Mike nodded, and Bellenger and Dale Reid herded Peter and me toward it, their guns pressed into our backs. Mike walked alongside me.

"You know, every now and then when we have one of these forest fires," he said in a friendly voice, "some moron decides he just has to get to the other side of the fire and finds a back road through the restricted zone. We got us a big one going out there now, and there must be two dozen little roads going in and out of that area. Some of them are totally unmarked and nobody's got the men to spare to watch them all."

"Open the trunk," Bellenger called to Bert, who hopped out of the driver's seat to comply.

"A few years ago," Mike continued, "this nice young tourist family got trapped between two arms of the fire when the wind shifted, and roasted to death right inside their car. Made the papers all over the state—maybe you read about it."

I had, but I wasn't about to give Mike McCutcheon the satisfaction of telling him that.

"Get in there, honey," Bellenger said, pointing at the open trunk. "This is a kind of game. When you get there, it's against the rules to know where you are." I climbed into the trunk space and scooted over as much as possible to one side. Peter climbed in next to me and the lid slammed down. Someone started the car engine and we began to roll.

Inside was hot blackness and the smell of exhaust. "I'm sorry I got us killed," I said to Peter. "I should have run the other way."

Peter put out a hand in the dark and held mine. "We're not dead yet," he said.

I decided against mentioning that it was pretty much a technicality at this point. I lay against the scratchy trunk carpeting like a corpse, my emotional responses shutting down like a broken machine, probably a defense mechanism against fear.

"How you doin' back there, honey?" Bellenger called from the front of the car, his voice somewhat muffled by the backseat, but unfortunately quite understandable. "I've got something real special planned for you when we get where we're going." He laughed unpleasantly. "We're going to get to know each other real well. Dale and those other guys are going to give us a little while alone together. Won't that be nice?"

I discovered I could still feel fear. And hate.

The car twisted and turned on the mountain roads. I listened for sounds that might identify our route, but Bellenger was avoiding the highway and main roads. Now and again I heard Dale direct him onto a side road, and we'd turn off in another direction and the twisting would begin again. I was more than a little sick to my stomach, and short on oxygen, and when we got where we were going, someone was going to arrange for us to burn to death. After Craig Bellenger got through with me, that is.

I've led a pretty uneventful life, all things considered. I moved around a lot as a kid, but I had a relatively peaceful childhood with reasonably well-balanced parents and no major complaints outside of a certain rootlessness, which I tried to solve by moving to a middle-sized town in northern California and refusing to move again for the next fourteen years.

Somewhere around the time I turned twenty-nine, a little more than three years ago, I divorced my husband and changed jobs, but even working for Baronian Investigations had not exactly been a thrill a minute. In between the occasional satisfying conclusion to a tough case followed by the occasional champagne celebration with Jake Baronian, were days and weeks and months of routine insurance surveillance and industrial undercover work. These kinds of jobs are so disagreeable that they usually don't get included in the TV shows. They consisted of roughly ninety percent boredom and ten percent downright unpleasantness, but they were almost never actually life-threatening.

It was only the past month or so that anyone had ever made a serious threat against my life, and only a little more recently than that had I been forced to make a choice between my life and the life of another. Having that choice woke up a spirit of survival in me that most people never find.

I still had that spirit, I discovered, poking around for it like a tongue on a sore tooth and finding it hot and painful in my chest. I wanted to live. I wanted Peter to live. What could I possibly do to assure that?

"Take this one coming up on the left," Dale said from the front seat, and the car turned and left the pavement behind, bouncing into and out of ruts and potholes. My head thumped against something hard. Biting back a yelp, I put my free hand up to the new bruise and discovered my duffel bag.

Ever since I'd found myself facedown on a dead man's chest with a pit bull trying to eat my face, I'd been feeling like a total fool for not carrying my gun. No matter what personal changes I'd been forced to go through on account of using it against another human being, I'd lost sight of a very important principle: alive is better than dead. Now I'd been given another chance to prove whether I believed it.

I reached up and found the zipper that closed the end compartment of the bag. Slowly, I unzipped the opening enough to get my hand inside. The feel of cold, hard steel was the most welcome sensation imaginable.

The gun was cocked and loaded with the safety on, the way Jake insisted I carry it. The time needed to put the first bullet in the chamber, Jake felt, could be the time you needed to save your life. I pulled the Walther from the bag and pressed it against me. We'd had our differences in the past, but two lives were on the line, and it was time to kiss and make up.

I gave Peter's hand a reassuring squeeze. Then I pulled it over and closed it over the Walther and held onto him as he recoiled predictably. "Alive," I said to him, trying to make my voice reach over the noise of the unpaved road, "is better than dead."

"No secrets back there," Bellenger called out. "I don't want to hear any more talk."

In a few minutes, the car slowed and stopped. The heat was almost unbearable by now, and I had to will my hands to stop shaking.

I heard the car doors slam, then Bellenger's voice outside the trunk. "I'm going to open this up, now, and I've got a gun on you, so don't try anything or you'll just be dead sooner."

The key turned in the trunk. "You get out first," I whispered to Peter, "and stand clear." The lid went up. There was some light from the headlights back here, but it was still pretty dark. The smell of smoke burned my nose and throat, and the heat was intense. I could see the fire, not nearly far enough away, and hear the tortured roar it made. I turned on my side, holding my left hand under me, pretending to be immobilized with fear. It wasn't all that far a reach, really.

"Okay, get on out of there, queer-lover," I heard Dale say. Peter stepped out of the trunk slowly, his legs unsteady. He backed away a couple of steps toward Dale, who poked him with his gun. "Not so close, asshole," Dale complained. He was visibly nervous about this whole thing, and I hoped he was keeping a real loose grip on the trigger.

Bert Trout's truck pulled up a little way behind us. The lights stayed on, turning Craig Bellenger into a looming silhouette surrounded by whirling smoke.

"You're next, sweetheart," said Bellenger. I looked up at him and whimpered. He reached forward with his left hand to grab me, letting the gun drop a bit.

I rolled onto my back and put four shots into his chest.

CHAPTER 29

BELLENGER DROPPED LIKE A STONE, FALLING ONTO MY LEGS and chest. Silvertip. 32 shells have a lot of stopping power for their size, but not enough force to push a grown man's body off its center of gravity. I tried to pull away, but there was no room to maneuver.

In the glare of Bert's headlights I saw Peter drop down and bring his right elbow up into Dale's crotch. Dale's gun clattered to the ground, followed by Dale. He screamed and Peter dove for the gun.

Bert was out of his truck in an instant, bringing his gun up to fire as he ran. I lifted my arms over Bellenger and tried to lead Bert's running figure. My shot went wide. He got off a burst, which slammed into the trunk lid a foot over my head.

Peter picked up Dale's gun and stitched the ground in front of Bert with bullet holes.

"Drop your weapon, Bert!" someone shouted, and Jim Lauderdale, pistol drawn and aimed at Bert's back, stepped out of the passenger side of the truck.

Bert turned his head and looked at Lauderdale over his shoulder as though he'd lost his mind.

Lauderdale produced a badge from inside his shirt and held it high. "James Lauderdale, United States Justice Department."

Bert spun around and fired. Lauderdale dropped to the ground and got off three expert shots. Bert fell where he stood, bleeding out rapidly from three sizable holes in his back.

I sank back into the trunk under Craig Bellenger's dead weight and thought about passing out.

The sky was a blistering orange color on three sides of us, a bit less so in the direction from which we had come. Lauderdale raced Bert Trout's truck over the rutted dirt track, back toward the main road. Dale Reid was handcuffed in the truck bed in the company of two corpses. He was not enjoying the experience, and let us know about it with a steady stream of curses that reached us even over the noise of the engine and the howling of the fire.

The forest was burning almost up to the right-hand side of the road, encouraged by a shift in the wind. Lauderdale hugged the left, hoping the natural firebreak would protect us long enough to find a side road leading away from the blaze.

Somewhere beyond us, on the unburned side, heavy machinery thundered, plowing down trees and creating a barrier of barren dirt to stop the spread of the fire on that side. If we could get that far, we could follow the roads the firefighters were using to get back to Cedar Ridge. Going overland was impossible—the trees and rocks were too thick to take a car through. Our only hope was to find a road.

I leaned against the passenger side door, blood soaking into my clothes, and watched trees burn.

"Don't worry about me, Peter," I said when I caught him staring at me. "I'm going to be fine." And I was.

I'd told Peter I didn't know if I could survive killing again. In a way, you *don't* survive a crisis situation of that magnitude, because every crucial act tears down and re-forms you, to some extent. The person faced with the decision whether or not to squeeze the trigger is not exactly the same as the person who feels the kick of the gun in her hand.

Craig Bellenger was dead, but I couldn't convince myself that the world would be a better place if Peter and I had died instead. The revulsion I felt for the act of homicide couldn't measure up to the alternative. I was glad he was dead, and if that meant I had to kill him, then I was glad of that, too.

Being glad I had killed a man made me feel like a murderer. I sighed, exhausted by following the mental trails, which led to more and more branching roads until I felt lost in the woods. There was no escaping the emotional consequences of such an act, but knowing it was justified was something to hold on to, so I did.

I looked across Peter at Jim Lauderdale, his face set in a mask of concentration on the task at hand—getting us out of the fire zone. Beneath that mask I could see other forces at work. Jim had killed for the first time tonight, and I knew something of what he was going through. Along with the sense of wrongdoing comes an unwelcome awareness of impending mortality. If death is that easy, your mind keeps asking, who's safe? The answer, of course, is: no one.

Jim had been placed undercover at the Sheriff's Department at the Castle Valley substation four months before. The Office of Special Investigations of the Justice Department had its eye on the American Rescue Coalition, and there were already signs that a number of sheriff's deputies and even some officers were involved in A.R.C. activities.

"They knew the real hotbed was nearer Cedar Ridge," Jim had told us, "but they didn't want me to become too familiar to the locals, so they had me stationed at the other end of the county." Jim had asked around discreetly and been referred to Craig Bellenger. When Bellenger felt he could be trusted, he was introduced to Mike McCutcheon.

"I was there Thursday night when Mike admitted he gave the order," he said. "I had plenty of evidence on a shitload of civil rights abuses, and I could have burned them right then on homicide and saved a lot of trouble, but Mike had been hinting around that he knew the identity of Andrew Weiss, and I really wanted that information."

"Mike knows who Andrew Weiss is?" It was hard to believe, but not impossible.

"At first I thought he was just shooting his mouth off," said Jim. "But he acted like a guy with the inside track, and he promised to bring Weiss to meet us when the time was right. I was trying to hold out for that."

How could Mike know Andrew Weiss? Was he that high up in the A.R.C. power structure? The thought was interrupted by the sight of a tree ahead of us starting to fall across the road. I pointed at it and shouted. If it fell in front of us, we'd never be able to get over it except on foot. If it fell *on* us, we'd be fried alive.

Jim gunned the motor and I reached up and grabbed the chicken strap above the door. Peter braced his hands against the dashboard. The tree fell toward us in stunning slow motion, trailing sparks and fire into the sky.

We hit a bump and the truck leaped into the air and brushed the lower branches of the tree as it fell. We came down on all four tires just beyond its resting place.

Dale Reid shrieked with fear, then returned to shouting obscenities and pounding his feet against the truck bed.

The tree shuddered as it impacted on the ground. Its top branches reached all the way across the road and ignited the dry grass on the other side.

The fire was generating its own wind now. It pushed a wall of unbearably hot air before it, and threatened to burn up every iota of oxygen. The smoke burned our lungs and our eyes. It was almost impossible now to see anything very clearly.

"Look! I think that's a road!" Peter yelled, wiping at his eyes with his shirt sleeve.

"You're right!" said Jim. He cut the wheel left onto an even smaller dirt track going away from the fire's leading edge. The truck's rear end careened around in the dirt and slammed into a granite boulder. Dale screamed. Jim righted the truck and continued down the road.

The road dipped and twisted dangerously, a one-lane dirt track overgrown with manzanita and pine seedlings pushing their way up between the tire ruts. Trees and rocks were too close for comfort on either side, but we could see the fire at our backs, and feel it, and hear its voice. Jim kept the speed up, hunched over the steering wheel, trying to see far enough ahead to avoid disaster. Disaster came anyway.

This had probably once been a fire road, but had not been maintained for many years. Spring rains from previous years had formed a seasonal creek across a low spot between two little rises, and a culvert put in to carry the flow had collapsed, leaving a three-foot-wide ditch running across the center of the road. Jim braked hard and the truck skidded on the dry dirt and pitched sideways into the ditch. There was a shriek of tearing metal, then silence.

I ended up on the high side, so I pushed the door open with both feet and crawled out. I jumped down to the ground and waited for Peter and Jim. "How far do you think the firefighters are?" I shouted above the sound of the fire. The rumble of bulldozers seemed to come from everywhere the fire didn't, and the fire was gaining on us.

Peter and Jim shook their heads, as disoriented as I was.

"Hey!" A shout from the side of the road. "Hey, don't leave without me!" Dale Reid had been thrown from the truck bed, and was crawling toward us, one foot dangling behind him in a way that made my stomach twist.

Jim and Peter ran to Dale and pulled him to a standing position. "Watch the foot! It's broken or sprained or something!" Dale cried.

The two men supported him between them and I brought up the rear. We made tracks down the road away from the fire, the truck, and the bodies of Bellenger and Bert Trout.

"I can't go this fast!" Dale yelled after a few yards. "You've got to slow down!"

"That fire isn't slowing down," Peter shouted, looking back over his shoulder.

"We could always leave you here," Jim offered.

Dale shut up and shuffled along, grunting with pain. I couldn't bring myself to feel too sorry for him.

There was a rush of superheated air like a hot cyclone, and the trees above us exploded. Hot pitch and cinders fell down on us like a rainstorm from Hell. I could no longer hear the noise from the fire line, only the hot roar of flames all around. I couldn't tell whether I was running away from the fire or into it. Peter stumbled under Dale's weight and went down on one knee. I lifted him up and we ran on—into safety or death, I didn't know.

I was dying for a breath of air. My lungs wanted to burst, drowning in heat. I thought about Tom Wynand's trick for staying cool in the heat. I would have laughed if I thought I could spare the breath. I could no longer see, and stumbled along beside Peter for a few steps before I lost consciousness between one step and the next and fell to the ground.

CHAPTER 30

"WHERE THE HELL DID YOU GUYS COME FROM?" SHOUTED A man's voice. Rough hands pulled me up and supported me. I felt myself floating above the ground, dreaming about Andrew Weiss, only now he had a face.

"You're going to be all right," said a young man's voice. I looked up into a pair of bright blue eyes in a face blackened with soot. One of the hands belonging to the face was taking my pulse, and the blue eyes checked the time on a watch to confirm the diagnosis.

"Your friends are fine too, except one of them has a broken foot, and everybody's got a few little burns." As if to illustrate, he pulled on a rubber glove, dabbed at my forearm with a sticky yellow salve, and placed a square of gauze over the spot. "You were lucky to get here alive."

"I know," I said, and realized how much talking hurt— my throat felt sandpapered. The sensation brought tears to my eyes, but I was grateful for the ability to talk, see, and breathe. "Do I look as bad as I feel?" I asked my benefactor.

"Oh no, ma'am. You look just fine." A flicker of a smile crossed his lips. "Well, you're a little dirty, but other than that . . . I'm Paul, by the way. I work for the C.D.F."

I gave him what must have been a blank look.

"California Department of Forestry. We're the ones who're going to put this sucker out while those Forest Service clowns have themselves a little campout in the woods."

"I hope so, Paul. How soon can we get out of here and back to Cedar Ridge?"

"There's a truck going into Sacramento in a few minutes," he said. "They're planning on putting you on it. I've checked you out the best I can, but you need to be seen by a doctor."

He capped the salve and discarded the glove in a fliptop pail. "You'll probably spend the rest of the night fighting off reporters. You guys barely missed being burnt to a crisp. That's the kind of story that sells newspapers."

I sat up on the cot where the firefighters had placed me a few minutes (hours?) earlier. "What time is it? I need to talk to Lauderdale," I said. "I can't go to Sacramento—I've got some unfinished business in Cedar Ridge." I pulled my legs over the side of the cot with some difficulty.

"It's about half-past midnight. You lie back down," Paul said. "I'll find Mr. Lauderdale."

Paul was back with Jim and Peter in half a minute. "We have to get back into town," I told them. "Mike McCutcheon may not live long enough for you to arrest him."

The C.D.F. truck dropped us at the Sheriff's Department, and after a quick, private conversation with the commander on duty, Jim had a sheriff's car for us to drive around in, and a rifle which he placed carefully in the trunk along with a small metal box.

Mike wasn't at his house, and the meeting house seemed the next best bet. We took advantage of the almost total absence of traffic to make top time getting there.

We pulled up just off the road, opposite the dog kennel. The house was dark, but two cars were pulled up in the yard. One was the battered Camaro I'd seen earlier, and the other was Tim Wynand's.

"You were right," Peter whispered beside me.

"Not because I wanted to be," I said. "I just put it all together after the fire—the way he talked about his vision for Cedar Ridge, the packages from Los Angeles, 'Information, not politics'—that kept cropping up. What Jim said about Mike knowing Andrew Weiss helped me put it all together."

I shook my head. This was not the outcome I'd hoped for. "Now what do we do?" I asked.

"We take out the security system," said Jim.

He opened the trunk of the car and removed the little box and the rifle. "Go ahead," he said, handing me the box.

I opened it carefully. Inside, nested in gray foam rubber, were four red-flagged tranquilizer darts.

I handed one to Jim and he loaded it into the dart rifle and popped up a jumbo scope. A dancing red light appeared against the house, then steadied and headed for the kennel as Jim leaned across the hood, bracing himself on both elbows.

The dogs paced, growling and peering out through the wire. The red dot came to rest on the broad chest of the nearest dog, and the rifle coughed. The dog whined once and fell to the ground. The remaining dog sniffed its companion and resumed pacing.

I handed Jim another dart. The dog paused in its pacing to sniff the air. The red light danced along its flank. Jim squeezed the trigger. The dog jumped up and collapsed in a heap on the ground.

I could hear Peter's sigh of relief, even over my own. Jim slid the rifle inside the car window and retrieved a shotgun from the dashboard. His hands shook a little.

"You may not have to use it," I offered.

"But if I have to, I will," he said.

"I know." I still had the Walther, tucked into the back of my jeans, and I now had no doubt what I'd do if confronted with a life-or-death situation. The knowledge gave me a sort of grim satisfaction that I wasn't sure how to accept.

"Do you want to carry this?" Jim held out a nine millimeter Beretta to Peter. It was the pistol he'd used to kill Bert Trout.

I had seen Peter pick up a gun once tonight, and I wasn't sure if I wanted him to do it again. I kept my face impassive, hoping he wouldn't take a cue from me one way or another.

He held out his hand and took the gun. "Thanks," he said. I hugged him impulsively. "I know what this is costing you," I whispered. "I don't want you to use it unless you want to. Just look like you'll use it."

Peter smiled at me. "I think I know more about myself tonight than I've ever understood before. Don't worry about what I'll do or what I won't do."

"I won't."

Jim led the way as we walked quietly toward the house. The front windows were open to the night air, and voices were coming from the back of the house, one too quiet to make out the individual words, one clearly frightened. "Just don't kill me," Mike McCutcheon pleaded. "You don't have to kill me."

"Around the back," Jim whispered, and we followed him around the kennel side of the house. Just behind the kennel was a back door. It was ajar, and a dim light showed from the next room.

We walked into a small dark laundry room and paused at the threshold to the kitchen. Tim and Mike sat on opposite sides of an old chrome-and-Formica dining table, illuminated by a light coming from the propane stove. A bottle of expensive Scotch, half empty, stood on the table between them. Tim held a glass of liquor in one hand and a .357 Magnum in the other.

I've only read about the kind of holes that kind of weapon can put in a person, or for that matter a solid block of steel. At that range, Mike would be dead before he fell out of his chair.

"If you kill me, you kill everything," Mike was saying, leaning forward. "You'll be killing the A.R.C. Your dream of a better America will be deader than me."

Tim waved the gun in his direction and Mike sat back, rocking his chair on its chrome runners. "Everything I loved is dead," Tim said, and I realized he was drunk. The drink swayed in his hand and Scotch splashed onto the linoleum floor. "Cass Lowry is dead, and you killed her. If I don't kill you, I'm betraying her."

"How many times do I have to tell you, Tim? *Dale* killed her. *Dale* was driving the car. Why the fuck aren't you out looking for *him*?" His voice kept rising, on the edge of hysteria.

"He's dead, too," Tim said. "But you're first."

"You can't bring her back this way," Mike insisted. Sweat was pouring down his face and his breathing was more like sobs. "Didn't you always say in your letters to me—and even after you came to me—and told me who you were and how we were going to work together for Cedar Ridge and this whole country—didn't you always say 'The cause is more important than a life'?"

"Not *her* life!" Tim roared, standing up and pointing the gun at Mike's head. "Not *her* life!"

Jim reached around the doorjamb and switched on the overhead light. Tim wheeled and pointed the gun in our direction as Mike dove under the table. There was a roar of gunfire and Tim flew back against the stove, blood blossoming on his shirt and more blood spraying the wall behind him. He had enough time to look surprised and hurt before he died.

The three of us stood in the kitchen doorway, still in firing position. The clatter of a shotgun cartridge ejecting onto the floor was the only sound in the room until Mike McCutcheon's labored intake of breath from beneath the table.

"You're under arrest," Jim said to Mike as he pulled him out by his hair. "For felonious homicide, illegally possessing automatic weapons, and multiple violations of civil rights. If the Justice Department can come up with anything else, you're under arrest for that, too."

Mike scrambled to his feet to avoid having his hair pulled out by the roots. He sagged again when he saw Tim, a gaping red hole in his chest pouring blood out onto the floor. Jim escorted him around the growing red puddle and shoved him out the back door with one hand, the other still holding the shotgun leveled at Mike's back.

I took the Beretta away from Peter. The barrel was still warm to the touch. "Jim killed him," I said. "We just reacted."

Peter nodded, unable to take his eyes from Tim. "In a way, he killed her, too," he said quietly.

"In a way," I said, taking his arm and leading him out of the house. "Everyone who never stood up against men in hoods was responsible for Cass and a lot of other people who'd be alive today. We have to start from now, Peter. From right now."

"Yes," he said. "It's time to start living."

We rode to the Sheriff's Department with Jim and sat in a harshly lit room giving statements to the commander and the sheriff, who was called from home and showed up in a uniform and sheepskin-lined bedroom slippers. We sipped coffee from cardboard containers and felt adrenalin giving way to exhaustion. Finally, we were free to go.

Jim stayed to telephone the O.S.I., and Peter and I accepted a ride back to the house with a deputy who was full of questions we declined to answer about the shootout and the A.R.C. and was it true there were Department people involved, and what did we think was going to happen now? We thanked him for the ride and let ourselves into the darkened house, turning on lights as we went from room to room.

I looked down at myself. My hands and arms were covered with scratches and bandages and dirt and ashes. Blood dropped from my jeans and shirt onto the carpet in little black flakes, and I stank of death and the fear of death and the fire.

Peter nodded at me, looking down at himself. "I think we both need to wash up and have a drink," he said. "I'll take the upstairs bathroom and you can use the one down here."

I reached into the pocket of my jeans and found a crumpled-up piece of paper. I unrolled it and smiled when I re-read the message.

"First," I said, "I have to make a phone call."